IMPASSE

A UNIFORM AND LACE ROMANCE NOVELLA

TINA MAURINE

COPYRIGHT

Impasse

A Uniform & Lace Romance Novella

Tina Maurine

DEDICATION

To my sweet T. & K.
You kiddos rock!
Thanks for the joy you bring me every day...
I love you bigger than the universe.

To B.
How did I ever get so lucky?
With you, the world makes sense...
I love you forever.

To Mom
For being the kind of mom I strive to be everyday.
For being my best-friend... since forever.
I love you Momma!

Prologue

"Miss Renyols, the President and First Lady are ready to see you now."

I stood confidently and smoothed my hands over any creases that may have formed on the plain, conservative suit all of us in the security detail wore.

"Thank you, Ollie." I smiled warmly at Mr. Marsh, the President's personal assistant, as he opened the door to the Oval Office and gestured for me to enter before him. I approached Ethan and Kaitlyn West, who were seated on sofas gathered in an informal sitting arrangement in this office of such high prestige.

"Vette," the first lady rose and extended her hands out toward me, "both Ethan and I are so glad that you could find the time in your busy schedule to fit us in."

I took both of Kait's hands in mine and held them in friendly greeting. "Anytime either of you needs me, you know I'm here for you." I smiled largely and with the genuine warmth I felt for both her and the president.

"Miss Renyols, please take a seat. Kait always thinks I

have all the time in the world, and although I make time to prioritize my family, I really haven't any to spare."

I nodded to the president and took a seat across from him next to Ollie, who sat poised and ready to take notes on the legal pad he had open on his lap. I watched as President Ethan West took his wife Kait's hand in his. His eyes met hers in quiet support and provision. He nodded gently before they both turned their attention toward me.

"Vette," she began in a wavering voice, "I will have to be cutting back on the myriad of duties, projects, and commitments I've been pouring myself into these past years. You've worked for us as head of our son, Davien's, security detail for just under a year, and I..."

"We," the president interrupted her, "will be having you take on added duties with regard to Davien."

"Yes," Kait went on, "what Ethan is trying to say... is that I'm sick."

Oh my god, Kait! Please...this can't be true...

"Very sick," the president added.

"We have interviewed for nannies we thought Davien might respect and click with, but even amongst the best applicants, we found fault." She shook her head and the two of them caught each other's eyes before she continued. "Vette, I have stage four cancer, and although we are going to fight this with the best treatments from the best doctors, my prognosis is grave."

No, no, no, no, no! This can't be true.

"Don't say that bab... err, Kaitlyn. You can beat this. You know I'll spare no expense."

"Shh, Ethan, my love. Now's not the time to rehash this..." she briefly looked over at me as she squeezed his hand, "we have company." They held each other's gaze for a time, before the president diverted his attention to me.

"Miss Renyols, we—Kait and I—feel that because Davien is nearly seventeen, and because you are with him practically every minute of every day anyways... that perhaps you'd consider being his pseudo-nanny, so to speak?"

Hell NO! There's no fucking way, guys... no way. I don't want to have to manage Davien. Noooo fucking way... besides...

"Mrs. West..."

"Kait, *please*," she said with quiet adamancy.

I nodded, "Kait, I can't be..."

"You can," the president interjected gruffly, "and will if you'd like to keep this assignment."

Well... then fuck this job. I thought indignantly, then noticed the first lady. She shot her husband one of *those* looks.

"Please, Vette. I'd... we'd feel much better knowing that someone who already has his best interests at heart, someone who already knows the... shall we say, weaknesses in character and behavioral traits," she chuckled, "would be looking after him in my absence."

I stood and walked to the window in quiet reflection.

How the fuck am I supposed to make her understand that I am NOT mom material? I can't be watching after him! Davien no less! He's NOT an easy charge. Besides, I'm too messed up to deal with anyone else's shit. I crossed my arms as thoughts of my own childhood bombarded my mind, each more painful and harder to reflect on than the last. *I can't do it. I was never meant to be a mom, and after Iraq, I just... I can't.*

I turned slowly and walked back to where they were sitting, "Mr. President, Kait, I really think after careful consideration, that both of you, Davien, ...and for all parties involved, I'd best serve your family by remaining as *only* head of his security detail."

"*THAT'S* not an option."

"Ethan, please." Kait looked at him pointedly, then patted his leg in a quiet, *I've got this* gesture.

"Respectfully, I am NOT mom material." I could feel my heart begin to race and my anxiety was climbing at the thought that I'd either be fired or forced to take on these extra duties that I most certainly did *not* want.

"Ethan and I are not asking you to be Davien's *mom.*" The harshness with which she spat 'mom' indicated I'd clearly offended her sensibilities. "You know he's mostly grown. We don't need an official 'nanny', more of a bodyguard with the implication that you'll also keep him from scandalous situations. We just need someone to be there for him; someone he can come to or talk to... You already shadow him and keep him out of trouble. This would just be double-insurance you'd keep him out of *all* kinds of trouble... especially the kind of trouble reckless boys his age get into."

I nodded slowly as I listened to her plea. "Please forgive me for using the term mom. I only meant I'm not a nurturer. It goes without saying that you ARE and forever will be, Davien's only mother. It's just... and please don't take any offense, but I am not interested in taking on this level of responsibility and with it, the added stress and anxiety it would cause me." I hurriedly added, "I hope you understand."

"I hate to say this, but I told you so."

YOU told her so? What exactly did you tell her about me? Nice to know I've busted my ass; and now, after all this time to find out you have reservations about me. Nice. Real fucking nice...

"However do you mean, Ethan? Told me what?"

"That we'd be taking a risk by hiring her for this detail. She's clearly not the person that we banked on her being."

I'm not the person...? "I'm sorry..." I butted in with no regard to the fact that the president was speaking to his first lady. "What do you mean I'm not who you counted on me being?" my voice broke. "I've worked 24-7 for you guys, followed Davien to the ends of the map and then some..." I laughed. *If only they'd known the places and situations I'd pulled him out of.* "How am I *not* who you thought you'd hired."

The president spoke first, "Your military history

clearly outlines the trauma you've suffered and the resulting PTSD. I felt it was a deal-breaker. Seems I was right."

"Ethan..." Kait shook her head, then looked at me before continuing. "Vette, if it were a deal-breaker, you wouldn't be here. I loved your file and how you've rebounded from a past riddled with tribulations... it IS, after all, our pasts who make us who we are today."

I nodded and smiled at her.

"Please reconsider." Again, her voice wavered. "I'm going to die, Vette. Please don't let me worry for the next few weeks or months about who my son will have to go to if he needs an ear, or a friend he can count on in absence. Your job detail really won't change much, except for if he needs anything outside of your current job duties, they'd fall under the pseudo-nanny detail... if that makes any sense?" She quickly added, "He's not a child, so it wouldn't be for much longer."

I nodded again and stood, quietly absorbing what I'd just heard. I did love Kait and her family. "In that case," I said heavily and with audible uncertainty, "it would be my pleasure to attend to Davien and *all* his needs, not just the ones pertaining to his security." I heard the president grumble under his breath, but Kait jumped up and embraced me in a tight hug.

"Oh thank you, Vette! Thank you so much for caring after my baby. You have no idea what this means to me." Her voice broke and she released a quiet sob.

You're the only reason that I've stuck around this long. I thought, looking at the seemingly displeased president. *When aren't you unhappy?* I smiled. *Oh, that's right, when you're calling the shots and not...* "Kait," I whispered as we held each other, "so long as I'm here looking after Davien, you have *nothing* to worry about."

Chapter One

I shifted uncomfortably on the hard clinic couch, moving the bone-ivory pillow from behind my back and settling against the gold wool.

"Vette, why do you think President West hired you to run the security detail for his son?"

I shrugged nonchalantly at the shrink. "I'm guessing he received my file from the CIA—honestly, I've never given it much thought... although to say I was surprised would be a lie. I was an INTEL officer with the ISA." I paused, waiting for her to acknowledge the accomplishment. *Nothing.* "It is the highest division of intelligence for the US military..." *Still nothing from her. What the fuck?*

"Dr. Thorne, following my military service, I was at the top of my game. As a result, one of the top private military companies—one that is contracted with the US government—hired me as a private security contractor, a mercenary. With them, I completed missions that officially never existed. I have a top security clearance, tactical training, vigor and brazenness. I am fully qualified—overqualified—to run after a punk kid."

I watched as my president-mandated therapist, Belle Thorne, scratched on her note pad for my official, bi-annual review.

Hope that's a new pen! I thought arrogantly, used to her making notes during our sessions. *Although this seems like more than usual, even for you.*

"So, you feel qualified for the position?"

"I do."

"In spite of your clinical diagnosis of PTSD?"

"Belle..."

She interrupted me. "Dr. Thorne, please."

I watched her make a few more scratch marks on her notepad.

"Belle, we've done this since Kaitlyn passed from ovarian cancer. Many times in the past months. Can we possibly just call it good today?"

"Officer Renyols, you know what would make it a good day? You not fighting me. You respecting that, while *you* may feel fine, it remains up to me and my professional opinion whether I sign off if you're fit for duty."

"I was merely saying..."

"I'm saying, respectfully *let me* do my job. Upsetting me will not garner the results you desire."

I nodded, resigned.

"Tell me; how do you feel about the first lady's passing?"

I sighed. *This is such an incredible waste of time.* "Kait was educated, eloquent, and kind. It was her kindness that softened the public—and her husband. She did more for her humanitarian causes than most do in their lifetime."

"Tell me about this; is this why you don't mind the dual roles as Davien's head of security and his pseudo-nanny?"

"She had always been inordinately kind to me. She had found out—I guess from my file—what happened in Iraq. At first, I was irked that she knew the details of that day," I paused to draw in a long, cleansing breath, "the day the terrorists infiltrated our base." I shuddered involuntarily, noticing Thorne having a field-day of this in her notepad. "But, once I saw her humanitarian efforts, I just innately knew she was one of the kindest people I'd ever had the pleasure of working for." I laughed. "Although that doesn't say a lot, considering the motley crews I've worked with."

I took a long draw from tall glass tumbler she'd placed on the table beside the couch. Ever since I'd asked for a glass of water that first visit with her, she'd had one sitting there for me. It had taken a year of going first bi-monthly, then monthly and now every six months for me to appreciate the kind gesture. "Kait's efforts were international in their spread and varied. She saw a need for sanitary women's products in numerous third-world countries and got them what they needed. She personally fitted kids and adults in Ecuador with hearing aids. She saw the need for schools in Kenya and made sure they were built. Infants needed shots in Uganda—she had them shipped."

I took a moment to reflect on her question: *How do I feel about caring for all things Davien? All things, especially outside of my title as Head of Security.* "You know, when Ethan and Kait hired me, it was because she had so many commitments regarding her humanitarian efforts, and she needed a hand in watching over Davien in her absence." I paused, shifting my weight on the couch.

"As terrible as it was—her passing—to me it is was not a surprise. When you're that sick, and working that hard, something has to give. She literally gave her life trying to do right by as many people as possible. So I guess I felt like, because she did so much for everyone else, the least I could do was care for her son in her absence."

Thorne flipped through her notes, "You mentioned a few sessions back that your best friend from childhood had the same form of cancer. How's she doing with her treatment?"

"You know," I went on, deep in thought, ignoring the question. "Kaitlyn West's death rocked the White House. She blew in like a hurricane, upending the old, classical décor, making it modern and warm. It's impossible to walk through the halls or wander through the rooms of their personal residence and not feel her presence in every one of them. Sad, really. She is so greatly missed."

"Vette? Vette."

I blinked, startled to find that she was questioning me.

"We're almost out of time, and I have to say—off the record—that your PTSD seems to have been re-triggered."

I didn't say anything... you don't have any proof. "Why," I commented lamely, "would you say that?"

"Vette," she said thoughtfully, rubbing the back-end of the pen over her bottom lip, "it's my job."

"But what did I say that makes you think it has... because it hasn't. I mean, my PTSD is controlled. I'm under control."

"PTSD is never fully controlled," she said warmly. "And, it's not what you said, so much as how you said it. How you communicate, and your body-language when you spoke." She smiled at me, hoping I'd lower the wall I'd just thrown up. "How defensive you are when I bring it up... just for an example."

"I'm *fine* Dr. Thorne." I said icily, ready to stand and leave. *You don't know shit about me... nothing that I don't want for you to know.*

She set her notepad down. "How do you feel working for such a hard-hitting man as President Ethan West?"

"Well," I stated in a deadpan voice, "he's easily 6'4" tall, broad-shouldered and his stature commands the same presence as his attitude. He is the Commander in Chief, and 'commander' fits his personality to a tee. He commands respect and is official in all of his dealings— personal and relating to the public office he holds so dearly. That is, except when it came to the first lady." I shifted my weight again, trying to get comfortable on the hard, wool couch, leaning forward, my elbows on my pantsuit-clad thighs.

"Around Kait, he was a whole different man; that is, when he wasn't in front of his adoring public. He won by a landslide, which I'm sure you know—the biggest in history—and not from a sleazy election either. People just believed in his abilities, and with his military experience to back it, and with Kait at his side, the American people rallied behind him. It's hard not to. Rally behind him I mean." I clasped my hands together and took another cleansing breath. I greatly disliked talking about Kait— and pretty much all things—with people like Thorne.

I looked her dead in the eyes, "So, to answer your question, I am honored to be working for the president. True soldiers are found in the trenches with their men, and I know President West is fighting the good fight... that's all I can ask of him and my team."

Dr. Belle Thorne nodded. She sat with her hands grasping each other as she rubbed the knuckles. Picking up her notebook, she unfolded a piece of paper and scrawled her name at the bottom. "I am clearing you for continued duty, Officer Renyols, but I want to see you back in here at the beginning of next month."

She opened her calendar, "Let's say the week after you get back from Davien's little birthday trip—sound like a plan?"

I nodded.

"But during the interim, I want you to journal."

Fuck me. "I'm sorry, what was that?"

She eyed me keenly, her eyebrow cocked.

"Sorry, but really? You want me to fucking journal? How often?"

"Ideally at the end of each day."

I laughed, and a snort escaped. "Well, that's *NOT* going to happen. I can tell you that much."

She didn't budge an inch. "I'd like for you to try."

"Thorne, I am all too well aware that President Ethan West hired me to run the security detail for his son. I know the role I was hired to fill was more than simply a personal bodyguard; I was hired to *care* for his son." I stood to leave. "He hired me knowing my history; the same history that was in my file, which hasn't changed, and neither has my mission or assignment. I was capable then and am no less capable now. No amount of journaling will change that." I glanced at my watch. "I really do need to be getting back. If you'll excuse me?"

Dr. Belle Thorne sighed and stood resolutely, smoothing her hands down her suit-like shift. "Vette, you're obviously one of the best in your field; otherwise, President West wouldn't have retained your services. However, you need to know that continuing to push the past under that façade you front will only work for a measured length of time. Eventually, even the best façades crack without care."

I nodded and extended my hand, "Thanks for your professional opinion, but I'm fine. Really." I shook her hand and smiled, then confidently strode toward the door. *Fuck. There's an hour of my life I'll never get back.*

"Officer Renyols?"

My eyes lifted from my steno-notepad, aka journal, as I laid my Parker fountain pen down on the page. It had been a gift from Ethan soon after Kait's death, to help me remember her by. He'd said Kait had developed a love of writing after first receiving a similar pen. He'd hoped I'd develop the same love for writing, and he'd suggested I'd have lots of time on my hands, waiting around on his son. I'd found it sweet that he'd known how close she and I had become during her fight.

"Yes?" I asked Foster Black, a member of my security staff.

"Davien has requested to go out."

"It's two-thirty in the morning. Where's he think he's going this late?" I grumbled.

Black shrugged his shoulders. "Damn kid. Maybe you can talk some sense into him. God knows I've spent the last ten minutes trying, and the arrogant little shit told me to take a hike... to get you." He laughed sardonically.

I nodded as I stood from the large table in the first family's informal dining room where I loved to journal.

There's just something about this room that I find comforting, even more than my own quarters, I thought, tightening the satin sash of my favorite robe I'd thrown on over my satin pajamas earlier.

"Thanks, Foster. I'll handle him. There's no way I'm going out this late, especially since we fly out in a few hours." I smiled warmly at him. "Go get a few hours of sleep. I'll need you ready and roaring first thing in the morning."

"Rodger that, Vette."

I cringed inwardly. Usually, my name didn't garner that response from me anymore, but when Foster used it, something about the way he said it stirred up memories of my dad. *My father. He was a hard one, just like Ethan was around everyone except Kait. He's harder than most with Davien.* I shook my head. *The only thing my dad had a soft spot for was his Corvette collection. Too bad he named me after them. They became a constant reminder that they were the apple of his eye, instead of me, his daughter.*

I walked silently through the corridors. Eerie light shone through the Venetians and other large-paned windows as I passed them, my feet padding softly on the eclectic collection of Persian rugs, some new, and some old, which populated the herringbone wooden floors. I nodded casually to the members of my staff who roamed the passageways on their twice-hourly security checks. Only those who lived within these walls knew the schedule.

I looked regretfully as I passed the door to the Treaty Room, which President West had redone for me as my private suite. Oh, how I wished I was ensconced in my down comforter instead of this shit-storm I was walking into.

I paused in front of the Lincoln Bedroom—Davien's apartment—right next door to my suite. I raised my deceivingly delicate hand—I could lay any grown man out with only the use of my hands and the Eastern martial art skills I'd become an expert in—to rap lightly on the impressive door, just as it swung open.

"Jeezus, Davien! Give me a fucking heart attack why don't you?" *Before my tour in Iraq, I was never this jumpy...*

He laughed maniacally, stepping aside to allow me entrance.

"How'd you know I was there?" I inquired as I stepped inside his bedroom.

"I ordered Officer Cruz to inform me when he saw you, and I just received the call."

Later, I'll have to remind Cruz who he takes orders from.

He winked. "So, Foster told you I wanted to go out?"

I leaned my shoulder against the wall by the impressive double doors, my face blank.

"So," he snapped, "why the fuck aren't you ready?"

I smirked arrogantly. *No* way *am I going out this late.* "Davien," I replied, trying to sound firm but unable to suppress a sigh, "it's too late."

He opened his mouth to argue, but I didn't give him a chance.

"Your father hired me to watch over you…"

"You're not my mom," he interjected angrily, *and drunkenly,* I noted. "Do your fucking job and take me out." He swerved toward me haphazardly, bumping his hip on a decorative table along the wall and cursing under his breath.

I watched with mild amusement and annoyance. *At thirty-four I'm too fucking old to be babysitting. What was I thinking when I accepted this assignment? Oh yeah; it would've been career suicide to turn down First Family security detail. Hindsight's 20/20 though. I wish I'd considered how sorry for myself I'd feel three years in…*

"You're right. I'm not your mom, but I am in charge of your safety, and so I've decided going out is not in your best interest."

He stood barely two feet in front of me, his sea-blue eyes glaring at me indignantly. I challenged him back, pulling on my sash in a decisive, final manner.

"Do you have any idea how beautiful you are?"

His comment upended me; I couldn't have been any more startled than if he'd jumped out of a dark corner at me. "Davien…"

"No, really, Cori." He advanced on me so suddenly that short of pushing him on his ass, I had no way to make an evasive move. "Cori," he hummed it as it rolled provocatively off his lips, "I like it so much better than

Officer Renyols." His body was close enough to mine that I could feel his warmth.

"Davien," I warned.

He leaned in, bending his head so his lips fell at my temple. "Cori," he whispered, "I think it fits you better than Vette. I always have." His eyes locked onto mine, "Vette is too severe." He took my hands and held them out to my sides, so he could appraise me in my satin robe—clearly the wrong choice to visit my drunken charge in. "There's nothing beneath that robe that's as tough as Vette implies." He smiled flirtatiously.

I needed to put an end to this—*tonight*—before it went any farther. *Why haven't I stopped it yet?* "Davien, your father hired me to watch out for your best interests..." I protested, uncomfortable and cornered. I could feel that all too familiar panic response setting in. *Fucking PTSD!*

He interrupted me. "*This*, what you do to me... *IS* in my best interest." He pressed his six-foot two-inch frame against my five-foot six-inch athletic one. His firm, muscular chest pressed against my ample curves. "Cori," he moaned, desire lacing the syllable, "as of three hours ago, I'm officially a year past being a child."

I cleared my throat and writhed in an attempt to get out from between this sexy, virile nineteen-year-old and the heavy door at my back. "Davien, please!" My voice sounded desperate, nearly pleading. My heart was pounding, and my hands had grown sweaty. *I NEED to get out of here.* I looked toward the other exit, "I'm practically your mother," I argued, searching for a reason that he'd relate to. "I'm old enough to be your mother!"

"No, you're not," he stated arrogantly, "but even if you were... that would make you fifteen when you had me... and that's fucking sexy as hell."

"Jeezus, fuck..." the explicative fell out of my mouth. *What am I going to do with this kid?* This sexy as fuck, hard-bodied, aroused sex-machine who turned nineteen as of three hours ago, this kid—who wasn't much of a *kid* anymore—was doing things to me. I needed for it to stop. I tried pushing him away, but his sturdy frame held me captive against the door, and short of dropping him to his knees, which I didn't want to do on his birthday, I couldn't think of a way out.

My body jerked when he took his hand and placed it at my nape, gently tugging my black-violet hair to tilt my head up toward his. I tore my jade eyes from his mesmerizing, clear blue ones. *They're even more beautiful now that they're heated with passion... wait, no! What am I thinking?* "Davien," I pleaded again, "I'm, I'm..." I stuttered breathlessly, "I'm practically..."

"No. No, you're not," he rasped raggedly. "There's no way I'd do *this* to my mother." His lips descended. His hot, dry lips pressed against mine, encouraging me to allow his exploration. The hand at the base of my neck held me firmly. He dominated me, although not in the slightest bit offensively. His other hand sent a shudder through me as it cupped my ass, hiking my apex into his impressive arousal.

My hands, which had been arrested against his chest in a half-hearted, frozen push, snaked up around his neck and found refuge in his sun-highlighted, sandy brown waves. I pulled him deeper into me, as my body folded into his. My mouth parted, welcoming in his scotch-flavored tongue. He skillfully explored, lancing and diving into my depths, before retreating and grazing my lips with his, nipping and biting before delving back in. Our lips danced to the beat of our pounding hearts. Our bodies swayed scandalously to the rhythm thrumming deep within our chests.

When he eventually released his hold on me, my neck, my ass, my lips felt desolate. Cold. Vacant. He backed up a bit, and for the briefest of moments, a fleeting expression of awe and shock, as intense as I was feeling, swept across his face, before an arrogant smirk chased it away.

"Fuck me," he marveled.

I met his gaze unabashedly as the dizzying effect of the kiss left my senses.

"I'll be damned..." he muttered.

The crack of my hand connecting with his cheek resounded off the walls of his cavernous room. My hand smarted. "Don't," I grated evenly, "ever try that again." I pierced his eyes with a finality I somehow mustered, despite how my core fluttered. My apex had grown moist and ached for his touch, not to mention the heaving of my chest and erratic beat of my heart. *What's wrong with me? Maybe I should write this one down in my "journal" for Thorne to use in her psychoanalysis of me...*

I turned from him and opened the door. "Go. To. Bed, Davien." I gave him one final once-over, my eyes lingering a second too long on his pronounced, heavy desire, easily distinguishable as it strained between the textured fabric of his low-waisted cords and his muscular thigh. *Sweet Jeezus.*

I pulled the door closed with a click, walked hastily across the hallway to my bedroom, opened the door and closed it. I leaned against it heavily, sliding to the floor, my head hanging to rest worryingly on my knees. I closed my eyes, the unwanted image of an arrogant Davien, remained. I shook my head to clear my recollection... how his eyes had danced impishly. How his swollen lips had smiled as I'd all but stared at his erection. I couldn't shake the image from my mind. *Fuck me. What have I gotten myself into?*

Chapter Two

I stood outside the Oval Study, the large yellow room framed by the Truman Balcony. President West used it as an informal work space and meeting area. He was currently inside with Senator Gordon and her son, Connor, and of course the birthday boy, Davien. I didn't have to be there to know that the president was giving Davien the rules for the trip we were about to embark on, and that Senator Gordon was dishing them out to Connor in like fashion. The two boys had been hellions from the time they'd met around the age of eight or nine, at least from what I've heard, and very little has changed. Without exception, every time they 'hung out' together, there was trouble.

The door opened and Ollie Marsh, Mr. President's personal assistant, smiled my way. I could tell he had a thing for me, but he was too ordinary, to dignified and bland, to arouse me in any way. I mean, sure, we'd had a glass of wine here and there, but to see him as more than just a friend would be nearly impossible. He was not my type... just to, *nice.*

"Officer Renyols, President West requests your presence."

I smiled and nodded as I walked through the door he held open for me. In passing, I noted the two upholstered sofas. If memory serves, Laura Bush redesigned the room during her term in the White House. The senator and her son were on the sofa to my right. I sat down opposite President West and Ollie, joining Davien. The little shit had his legs splayed wide, slouched as he rested the back of his head on the sofa cushion nonchalantly.

I hope that hangover hurts... bet you don't even remember last night. I shrugged it off, but the thought of him not remembering our kiss stung a little. It would take me awhile to get past the feelings he stirred deep within me.

"Officer Renyols?"

My eyes snapped in the direction the voice had come from. *Fuck!* I looked from the president, to the senator, back to the president and on to Ollie. I sought the assistant's eyes, imploring him for help.

Ollie nodded in my direction. "President West asked you if you needed a larger security detail to cover both boys, as the original travel plan didn't have Connor in it."

"Oh, yes. Of course." I paused, took a deep breath and turned to look at Davien, who sat there in smug, arrogant silence, smirking at my lack of focus. I narrowed my eyes at him ever so slightly before redirecting my attention to the matters at hand. "On second thought, Mr. President, I am confident with the security plan we have in place. We've background checked the staff at the Coco Bodu Hithi Resort, and this morning, I have confirmation that the Coco Residence, where we'll be staying, has been completely swept and any vacationers have been background checked as well. There is no immediate threat. As of two hours ago, the plane's flight plan has been approved and the plane prepped for the flight to the Maldives."

"That's wonderful, Vette," the president addressed me again by my cringe-worthy name. "That's why you're in the position you're in—you're fully capable and carry the tiniest detail out to completion."

I smiled at him and extended my hand in response to his outstretched one. He grasped it warmly, taking it in both hands.

His voice softened, "Take care of my boy. He's the only family I've got left."

"Yes, and who else is there to take over your legacy?" Senator Gordon chirped playfully. I smiled as I glanced from her to President West and saw definite chemistry there. *I wonder...*

I turned to my charge, "Get up, Davien. Have you packed yet?"

"Do you realize you haven't even wished me a happy birthday yet?" He eyed me mischievously.

"Happy Birthday, Davien." I cast him a haughty smirk of my own; not professional, but I was granted some leeway, seeing as how, for all intents and purposes, I also held the role of his nanny.

I paused from any further conversation with Davien until only he, Ollie and I remained in the room. "Have you packed yet?"

"No."

"Don't you think that's something that you should do?"

"Not really. All I need is what I'm wearing and a swimsuit... unless I chose to wear just my birthday suit? You'd like that wouldn't you... *Cori*?"

My eyes shot to Ollie, and his pointedly measured mine. "Davien, that's the complete *opposite* of what I'd like. Get up. Now, *please*." Frustration edged my voice and I could feel heat creeping up my cheeks. I'd never make a good mother. I hated dealing with this obstinate, bullshit behavior.

"Or *what*?" Davien crossed his legs defiantly and crossed his hands behind his head as though he meant to camp there for a while. "Do you plan to *smack* me, cause I have to say, from experience, I'd much prefer a good *spanking*."

Ollie choked as I heard him set his coffee mug down.

"Get your ass up. Now!"

"Okay, okay. Sheesh, boss. You could learn to have a little fun." He stood from the sofa, towering over me. Leaning in near to my ear, he whispered, "...about those birthday spankings?"

I pointed to the door. "Go pack. Now!"

I swear I heard him breathe me in as though he were smelling me, before he stood to his full height, he ran his tongue provocatively over his bottom lip and winked at me. "Ribbed latex, or lambskin?"

"I swear on my mother's grave…"

"I'm going." He strode toward the open door, pausing before he stepped into the passageway. Turning his head toward me, he shouted, "How about if I just pack both? That way we won't run out." I could hear him laughing as he headed to his apartment.

Condoms? Really? Little shit!

Chapter Three

We pulled out in a modest motorcade and headed to the president's plane; it wasn't Airforce One. President Ethan West was not a poor man by any stretch of the imagination and owned his own Gulfstream G650 jet. It was rumored that it had cost him, or his family—not sure of the specifics there—north of sixty-five million dollars, new.

Traffic was light between the morning and noontime rush hours, so we made it to the airport in record time and boarded the plane with zero unforeseen problems.

The plane engines were already starting, and after getting my charge situated, I took my seat in the forward cabin in one of the four club-arranged seats. I preferred this space to the mid-cabin, where the movie screen was always on. Here, I had my own table, 21-inch screen, and power-reclining leather seat. I also generally had my own flight attendant, as one worked the front and one the rear of the plane.

"Mind if I join you?"

I lifted my head, nodded and smiled at Officer Adrian Rogue. He took his seat across from me.

He and I had been stationed in Iraq together until my enlistment had ended. Then I had signed-on with a crew of independent security contractors for the US government. We'd always been close, and I have to admit, I wish more had happened than the one or two sizzling make-out sessions that still played through my mind when I wanted to satisfy myself. *Fuck. He was one hell of a kisser... and those hands... the size of his... erection.*

When I was hired by President West, he'd let me choose my security team, and I'd sought, and found, Adrian... who was currently dating one of Ollie's assistants.

"It's going to be a long week. Dav," he nodded toward the aft of the plane, "seems to be in rare form."

"Yeah, no kidding—the form of the devil incarnate." I laughed as another member from my team, Foster Black, joined us, taking a seat across the aisle, and the flight attendant began her safety spiel. I turned my devices to in-flight mode and crammed my ear buds into my ears, ready to hunker down for the nearly 15-hour flight to Dubai. We'd refuel there and continue on another two hours to the Maldives.

I glanced at Adrian, and, catching him watching me, flashed him a killer smile. I turned up the volume on my phone, letting the cool sounds of James Bay's song '*Let it go,*' wash over me, and let my mind drift.

Oh, how his hands splayed against my back. His hard erection ground against my intimates. I returned his kiss, deeply, passionately. Thoughts of the man who sat across from me flooded in. *Adrian was everything I wanted from a lover; attentive, adoring, and ardent. He was courageous, sexy, masculine... he was ALL MAN. He oozed sex appeal in the way he carried his strong, lean, muscular build, and in the way he commanded respect when he gave orders.* My best friend, Adrian, the *one* man I'd do anything for... filled my thoughts as I drifted off to sleep listening to Tom Walker's ballad, '*Fly Away with Me.*'

I rubbed my eyes; they were sore from tracking the satellite images—suspected terrorist targets—I'd been closely watching for the past eight hours on one screen and a Predator drone live feed video on another.

I stretched, repositioning the headphones I'd been using to listen to the Arabic, Pashto and Farsi chatter on the internet and in hacker forums. I needed a break, but since I was covering for Officer Julien Rowe, I just had to "embrace the suck;" the motto around here and accepted standard.

I'd returned from a tactical mission not even forty-eight hours ago, and immediately went in to debrief with the CO. My role in the ISA—Intelligence Support Activity Group— was to collect INTEL crucial to carrying out missions. Crucial to the Army's Delta Force and the Naval Special Warfare Development Group, since officially, SEAL Team 6, doesn't exist. They're the best and the brightest counterterrorism units around.

I had literally just made it back to my team's bunk when I'd been called in to cover for Rowe. Food poisoning. Just my luck. I'd staggered in, sleep deprived, filthy, and mentally exhausted.

"Officer Renyols, front and center, soldier."

I looked up, thrilled to have a reason to move from my station. Moving through the darkened tent past tables of computers, maps and light-tables with photos strewn across them, I reached the large table at the center of the room.

"Sir?" I responded.

And, that's when I saw him. Or rather, felt his energy...

How could anyone not? He was amped on adrenaline and testosterone—clearly jazzed about how well his team had carried out the mission. I stood front and center listening to him as he debriefed our commander. I faced this soldier, watching how he radiated masculinity and vibrated with energy. I was mesmerized. I wanted—needed—to know him. Intimately. I'd never been so drawn to someone I didn't know before.

Later that night I wandered into the base bar—if you could call a rough slew of tables and chairs haphazardly strewn on the desert sand, covered by a massive parachute a bar. The speakers were blaring, card games were going on and everyone was drinking, except for him and me.

I studied his breathtaking good looks and felt the electric

pull of his energy. I wanted Adrian and I'd be damned if it was going to happen while I was drunk. I discreetly watched him, as he nursed his one Jack & Coke for most of the hour. I was surprised with as hard as everyone else was throwing down.

He stood behind his second, Tanner Lyons—another hottie—watching the poker game. This table had to comprise one of the finest examples of masculinity... both in looks and military skill. These special ops guys were rugged, commanding, strong, and oozed raw sex appeal.

It took me several well-calculated minutes to make my way discreetly to him. Now, under the guise of watching the game, I stood directly behind him. I took a deep breath and slid my hand from the sinewy muscles at his upper back, down the taut ridges of his back. My delicate, slim fingers continued making their way down to the hard lines of his fine ass. He instantly stiffened. Every muscle in his body tightened, fight or flight, ready to spring.

"Hi," I whispered, more timidly than I'd imagined I'd sound. "I'm Vette."

He looked out the corner of his eye, taking me in, a sly smile etched on his handsome face. Reaching for me, suddenly pulling me from behind his shoulder, he wrapped his heavy, muscular arm around my athletic frame. I'd never wished harder than I did at this moment that I was sexy, if only to feel like I deserved his attention.

"You were in the TOC tent today." It wasn't a question. I nodded. "You were watching me." I nodded again, feeling

stupid; however, when he looked down from his impressive six foot plus height, my insecurities all went away. His eyes, warm chestnut pools of honey, weren't mocking or condescending. They shone with attraction.

"You know how I knew that?"

Shit! He'd noticed me as I'd all but undressed him with my eyes earlier!

"I noticed you," he rasped, as he gave me a squeeze, "your head bent over your work, the moment I walked in."

My attraction deepened, my jade eyes falling deeper into his honey depths. "Your raven-black hair shone nearly midnight violet, and when you looked up... fuck me," he admitted unabashedly, "I thought maybe the green-screen had reflected off your eyes, but now I can see they're just an amazing shade of green," he paused, studying me, "like the most perfect emeralds..." he uttered more to himself than to me as his voice softened and faded.

I was dumbfounded. I stood there awestruck, like an idiot. Do something, SAY SOMETHING I chastised myself, but nothing came to mind, except I blurted out, "Damn."

He'd laughed good-naturedly, "You can say that again. Hey, want to get out of here?" He squeezed me tighter to him as he began backing us around the crowd that gathered at the card table. It was as though he was my liege, and I followed him trustingly through the riotous midnight throngs.

We walked through the base, past the TOC and supply tents, past the infirmary and mess tents, on up the hill past the barrack tents until we'd reached the quieter, more secluded side of the base, where the special ops teams bunked. He led me to a wooden picnic table in front of a tent I presumed was his quarters, and climbed up on it, motioning me to join him.

"So, you're going to have to tell me more about yourself. You made, I'm sure you'd agree, a pretty brazen move." He paused while I situated myself next to him. Our knees touched as we faced each other. "But, you haven't said nearly a word. You're quite the paradox." He reached up and ran his hand through his dark waves, down across the whiskers on his jaw, and over his chin to his neck. Stroking his short beard, he cogitated, "Brazen and shy. Quite the anomaly around here."

"I, I..."

"Vette, right?" He didn't wait for me to confirm. "You know, I'm not going to bite." He smiled in the moonlight and the tension eased from my shoulders. I nodded.

"I don't usually—I don't EVER do that," I corrected myself.

"So, then," he paused as though searching for the right words, "why did you? I mean, if I weren't such a nice guy, that forward of a move—not to mention following me out here blindly like this—could've landed you in deep water." He chuckled. "Cause, and please don't take this the wrong way, but it certainly SEEMED like you've pulled off that kind of move before."

I smiled at him, relaxed now, knowing he wasn't going to pounce on me immediately, even if it was what I wanted. "I don't know what came over me; I mean, I don't even know your name. It's like, Petty Officer Rouse, or something?"

He burst out in loud laughter. "Rouse? Shit. I'd never hear the end of it if my parents had cursed me by bearing a last name like that. It's Adrian Rogue. First Class Adrian Rogue."

"Well, I'm Vette Renyols, and before you ask, yes, like Corvette. My dad collected them, loved them actually. So, naturally, when I was born, he named me after his most loved collection—his Corvettes." I shrugged and shifted myself more closely to him. My knee now lay across his right upper thigh.

"So," he cleared his throat and set his hand on my thigh, above my left knee, where it rested on his, "you grabbed my ass, remember? I'm still asking myself why a shy, mild-mannered girl such as yourself would do such a thing to a hardened war veteran like me." He chuckled. "I must be losing my edge."

"Shit, I'm not coming off that *mousy, am I?*"

"ABSOLUTELY."

I didn't expect him to say yes! What a slap in the face. Maybe I just need to go for it and show him he's wrong. That he doesn't have my number. *I drew in a deep breath for courage...* Fuck it!

I leaned in, reaching up behind his head, pulling him to me until I grazed his lips with mine. "I guess," I whispered nervously, "I finally saw something I wanted badly enough to go after it."

Adrian's eyes narrowed slightly, then darkened with desire. He took his right hand, his large, strong hand, and snaked it under my hair, finding its home at the base of my neck where he applied pressure, bringing me masterfully toward him. His lips met mine with hungry passion. He kissed me deftly, as his left arm reached around my back and pulled me to him in one swift move until I straddled him. I gasped through our kiss as I felt the hardness of his erection press firmly against the rear seam of my jeans. My knees fell over his hips on either side as the tops of my feet rested on the picnic table.

His hands skillfully skimmed up my sides. My skin drew taut and goose-bumped instantly, as his palms felt the weight of my breasts through my thin t-shirt. His hands were manic, moving masterfully across my breast, to my neck, while he deepened our kiss. His hands massaged their way down my back, one splaying across it, the other gripping my hip as his hard, pronounced arousal ground intimately against me.

"Vee?" I felt a strong calloused hand brush the hair from my cheek. "Vee, wake up."

My brain snapped from its deep contemplation. Lucidity flooded back through my consciousness, pulling me from my dream. *The same fucking dream; my agonizing memories, replayed in my mind like a broken record.*

I slowly opened my eyelids and stared into the honey-brown eyes of my best friend. "Adrian." I cleared my throat and shifted, uncomfortably aware of how close he was, afraid he'd see right through to my heart if I looked into his any longer.

"I figured I'd better wake you up before you said anything more incriminating in your sleep."

"No!" I gasped. "What did I say?"

"Well," he chuckled uncomfortably, "it wasn't so much *what* you were saying, but you were groaning and writhing quite a bit." His lips curved upward just slightly, as red crept up his cheeks.

"Oh my God." I paled and quickly closed my mouth.

He leaned in close, his lips mockingly flirtatious against my ear. "You weren't dreaming of me... were you?" He joked as he straightened and took the seat across the table from me.

"Hell no!" I hoped the vigor in my response didn't betray me.

"Well, that's too bad." He winked at me, knowing that I'd never take him seriously.

This is now how Adrian and I were. *Flirts.*

We'd made out that first night we'd met in Iraq, talking until the sun broke over the horizon, and then he'd been sent on a covert op two days later. His mission turned into weeks, then before long it was months since I'd seen him. I'll never forget though, one night I ran into him after he'd returned.

"Remember me?" I'd asked more timidly than I'd envisioned sounding. In an effort to redeem myself and appear more brazen, I'd run my hands from his shoulders down to his ass, as he stood overlooking a card game in the crowded base bar, Oasis. I immediately felt him tense, like the first night. I fought

a strong feeling of déjà vu. "I thought either you'd transferred or become a casualty of war, it's been so long since I've seen you," I joked playfully, although it was in bad taste. I tried to keep my cool, but what I really wanted to ask was, "Where have you been? Are you okay. Did you think of me at all?"

Adrian stood, steadfast. Unbudging. Seeming completely, and entirely disinterested. So, doing what any tossed chick in my position would do, I snugged up close to his form. "Adrian," I breathed into his ear, "I want you to fuck *me."*

That did the trick. No sooner had the words left my mouth than he'd grabbed my hand and led me briskly away from the loud music, darting off between two tents. Ensconced in the shadows, his lips hungrily met mine. His hands devoured the surface of my skin—roaming. Seeking and finding my sexy curves, he consumed me, taking liberties I'd dreamt these past long months he'd take.

It was dangerous how well he made my body crave him. His tongue delved into my mouth, tasting and teasing. His lips traced searing hot trails across my neck and collarbone, but his arousal. Fuck. *His cock goaded me, seeing if I'd make good on my earlier tease. I reveled in the attention. Adrian's attention. I teased his dick through his camis, relishing the feel of its hardness, his steel rod and pronounced helmet. All I wanted was him in my mouth, where I could savor the feel of him, revel in his musk.*

His lips retraced their exploration to my mouth and he kissed me deeply, roughly, lustfully before he froze. With a nearly painful sounding groan, he crammed his hands into his pockets and took a step back from me.

"Damn it, Vee! See what you do to me? Goddamn it!" He hung his head and I watched him kick at a mound of dirt. Then, clearing his throat harshly, he looked back up at me. "You and me. This is a mistake. Sorry." He waved his hands between us. "I know you were just flirting, this isn't who you are, and I took advantage of the bogus invitation." He sighed, "Jeezus, Vee. I haven't seen you in months, but I want you as badly as the first night we met... which is why we don't work."

"What do you mean we don't work? You were just HERE with me, right?" I could feel my insecurities surfacing, but anger pushed them aside.

"We can be friends..."

I interrupted him, "Friends is bullshit and you know it."

He shook his head and turned to leave.

"Wait!" my voice cracked from the emotion I was feeling and expressing so poorly.

"This," he gesticulated in the air between us "is why we can't be more than friends. Emotions get you killed out in the field. Caring for someone more than the mission will compromise it and my men." He moved toward me with conviction, sliding his arms around my waist and pulling my body against his hard lines. "I already care too much for you," he whispered painfully. "Nights when I was freezing in the Afghan mountains were only bearable because thoughts of you warmed my heart."

Fuck me.

"I don't even fucking know you—" he chided himself. "How ridiculous is that?"

"But you do. We shared so much... you know more about who I truly am than some of the friends I've had through high school."

"Vee, it's simple really," he said pushing me gently away, putting distance between us. "I'm already falling for you and that cannot happen while I am here on this set of orders." He was being honest, but I could tell it hurt him to shut me out. "You already mean more to me than I'd even believe was possible five months ago, and because of that, I can't draw you into the dark depths of my own vile reality. You'd get hurt in these hellish pits. You're too good, too pure, to exist down here with me. You deserve to be coveted, worshipped, and to do that would eventually ruin me."

"It doesn't have to be that way," I sobbed. "We're made for one another. I know you feel it too!" my voice hitched, seeking confirmation.

He shook his head adamantly. "To love you, Vee, would take me out of the head-space I need to be in every time I leave this base to carry out a covert op. I'd be too worried I wouldn't return to you. It would take my head out of the game." He pressed his palms to his temples, holding his head. "Fuck... this wasn't the plan. I wasn't supposed to meet you. Not now."

I heard him mumble something about knowing these were the rules before he took these orders, then he closed the distance he'd put between us, his head dipping so that his perfect lips met mine. He kissed me with such intensity, such caged passion that it stole the air from my lungs. His body molded to mine, his steel frame partnering with my subtle one. I felt his erection growing harder than I thought possible, pressing hungrily for its release, as his hands cupped my ass, then rested at my nape, driving our kiss. I fought for us, for life giving air, for him to realize we didn't need to be over before we began.

It was no use. He backed away from me, robbing me of my future. "Goddamn it, Vee. No more. God help my soul, to love you is to keep you from me. Mark my words, that's the last time I'll ever kiss you." He turned heel and strode off into the darkness between the tents.

I'd wandered, choking back silent sobs, swiping messily at the tears that streamed down my face, until I'd found myself at our picnic table. I lay down on it, staring up at the inky blackness above, only the brilliance of the stars to soothe me. I lay in the darkness and listened to the deep, stark sounds of silence. The thrumming of my heart was my only surety, my only comfort. As I listened to the rhythm, I nearly forgot that I'd died watching him walk away.

For months, I couldn't bear to see him. I'd spent my time meeting others for a random hook-up here or there, but even kissing them left me missing Adrian more, so I figured, what was the point? I'd made a point of staying away from his hangouts, and from the side of the base where his tent was.

Eventually, enough time passed and the raw cut he'd

made had scabbed over. I'd made it into the base bar and had joined a poker game with Adrian's second and close friend, Tanner Lyons. Not long after, Adrian joined us at the next buy-in. The game had been the vehicle that had steered us back onto the path for a close friendship that I still held dear to my heart. Someday, someday I still believed the stars would align themselves and we'd end up together... somehow.

Adrian thrummed on the table until I looked up at him in annoyance, my daydream shattered. "Yes?"

"I don't know, you seem... *off* somehow." He eyed me suspiciously. "Is everything ok?"

You mean besides not being able to get you off my mind? I shrugged.

"Come on now, you know you can talk to me, right, Vee?"

"I guess." I looked behind me to make sure no one was coming and nodded over to Foster, whose head slumped to one side while his chest rose and fell in deep, even breaths. "How long has he been out?"

"I don't know, maybe two or three hours. Why?"

I leaned in. "Cause, nobody, and I mean *NOBODY* can hear about this or I could lose my job."

Adrian raised an inquisitive eyebrow and leaned in, resting his elbows on the teak table between us. "You know, at least *you should know* with everything we've been through, that you can tell me anything, and I'd have your back."

I placed my head in my hands and shook it gently, "Oh Ade, it's bad. I don't know what I was thinking."

"Jeezus, Vee, what is it? You're starting to worry me." His eyes were shrouded, my trouble mirrored in his expression.

"Well, last night, Foster came and got me around 0230 to talk Davien out of wanting to go out." I looked out from my hands. Adrian was intently focused on me.

"And?"

"And, he made an advance."

Adrian sprang up from his seat, interrupting me. "That little piece of shit!"

"NO! No, it's not what you think."

"*Oh really*? Sure as fuck sounds like it."

"Okay, well at first it was..."

He cut me off again, "At first? Jeezus, Vee, what did you do?" He swiveled his chair and plopped down heavily.

"Well, he made an advance—pinned me against the door—and I don't know what he was thinking, or why, but then he kissed me." I reflected. "I was in a state of panic... you know how stressful situations can trigger me. I wasn't thinking..."

"And you let him?" Adrian interjected in loud disbelief.

"Jeezus, lower your voice!" I leaned back, cracked my

neck and shook out my shoulders. "He said I was beautiful," I lowered my voice even more, "and sexy." I shrugged, "It's been a long, *long* time Adrian, since..."

"He's a kid, Vee. He's the *PRESIDENT'S KID*."

"I know." I sighed heavily. "He's not *exactly* a *kid,* but I know. I did smack him, though. I told him never to do that again."

"Well, that's at least something, but where's your head at? This is a prestigious assignment, caring for and protecting the presidential family. If you betray their trust, and word gets out, you'll never work in this field again... *anywhere.*"

"I know. Trust me, I know. I feel terrible, but..."

"There's a but?" he interrupted, leaning in and taking my hands, pulling me across the table until my chest was forcefully against the edge, the table nestled into my armpits. "It's a good thing you're this security team's captain, because if I were in charge, this would be enough to..."

I eyed him, threateningly. "You'd fire me over this?" My eyes narrowed, and I seethed with anger. "Don't fucking push me, Adrian. We've been through a lot. You're a good soldier, but there's only so much *you* can deny me of... and wouldn't you say that you exceeded that limit back in Iraq?"

At that accusation, or maybe from the memory of any future *us* that he'd ended against my will so abruptly, he released my hands. I massaged my armpits.

"And if you ever threaten me again, or use force with me," I spat at him, "Adrian, *you'll* be the one without a job."

He shook his head as he stood from the table. "We're not done with this conversation," he leaned in on the table, close to where I was sitting, "and bringing up Iraq isn't fair. It's beneath you." He put his hand on my shoulder and eyed me, hurt lingering in his expression, before he strode from the forward cabin.

"Officer Renyols?"

I turned my head as I swiveled my chair to see who was addressing me. Connor was walking into the forward cabin, looking expectantly at me. I turned back around and began searching for my earbuds. After my heated discussion with Adrian, the last thing I wanted to do was talk to Davien's entitled, snobby friend... or that's at least how he'd always acted around me.

"Mind if I join you?"

I looked up at him, studying him really, before nodding. "Sure," I said sarcastically, "why not?"

He smiled at me, then ordered a ginger ale—using his manners, which surprised me greatly.

"Got a minute?" He sounded concerned. "It's about Davien... he's sleeping right now, and I know after we reach Dubai, he'll probably be up at least twenty-four hours before he needs to recharge—unless he passes out sooner," he joked easily.

The flight attendant walked in, and he turned to her,

reaching for his drink. "Thanks, this is exactly what the doctor ordered," and smiled at her politely.

So, he DOES have manners. Maybe I've always been wrong about him?

I crossed my hands in front of me. "So, Connor, you sound like you have something on your mind. What's up?" I smiled to encourage him, hoping he was one of those kids who could communicate clearly what he intended to say. It was selfish of me, but I was in no mood to try to decipher what he meant.

"Well, it's about Davien."

I nodded, waiting.

"Okay, I guess the easiest way to say it, is to just say it. Right?"

Again, I nodded. "Let me guess; when Davien comes to the Coco Bodu Hithi Resort, he has a casual hook-up he sees every time, and he wanted you to warn me that he'd be off schedule and not to worry." I looked at him smugly and cocked an eyebrow. "Am I right?" I winked. "Connor, I already know this... I'm his security, remember?

"No... that's not it, *not at all*." Connor sat back in his leather café-lounge chair, flagging the flight attendant down.

"Can I help you?"

"Sorry to bother you again, but I'd like two shots of Jose Cuervo, please," he requested, looking the flight attendant in her eyes.

"Two for me as well. Please." I smiled at her and mouthed, 'Thank you.'

"You know, he was totally right." He sat back in his chair and swiveled from side to side, pensively.

"Oh? Who? About what?"

"Davien." He paused, still gliding his leather seat meditatively from side to side. "Well, he said that you didn't think very highly of him, even after knowing him these past three years, and that you thought he was... how'd he put it?" He accepted his two single bottles, cracked one at the same time as I did, and we toasted in the air before each of us slammed back a shot. "He said that you considered him to be a kid and thought he was an, 'arrogant little shit'.

I sat back, stunned as I would've been if he'd gut-punched me. "I've never told him that."

"Does it really matter if you've said it? He still knows it, Cori... you don't mind if I call you, Cori, do you? Dav feels Vette sounds far too harsh for you, and I tend to agree."

"Actually, I'd prefer Vee." I leaned back in my chair, crossing my legs casually. "I've only ever let Davien call me Cori." My admission sounded feeble, even to my ears, so I added, "It's just something special he calls me; it would be strange if you used it is all."

Connor nodded, but scrunched his eyebrows in confusion. "So, if it's special, then you also feel like there's something *special* there? 'Cause… well, I mean, from what Dav's said, he's got it bad for you."

I shook my head slightly as I leaned forward, motioning for him to do the same. "Connor, it doesn't matter what, *if any*, personal feelings I have toward Davien, President West or anyone else he employs. He hired me to be Davien's personal bodyguard and 'moral-compass' so-to-speak. It's my job to keep him out of trouble, and to confuse my personal feelings with my professional responsibilities would be… irresponsible, to say the least."

"The very least," he agreed. "Okay, but it's like this. You know Dav… he's not exactly the committing type. I mean, you can't *not* know this, right?" I nodded. "You know he pretty much gets any girl that he decides he wants—always has, but especially now that he's *President West's* son." He leaned in even further. "But, have you noticed that he hasn't been going out the past few months, he's had me over and he's been—hanging out at home—with you? I mean, come on. It's the summer after his senior year, before he hits Columbia up in New York this September, and he's been staying home to watch movies. Which, coincidentally you watch with him." He opened his hands, as though presenting a gourmet meal. "Boom. In your face, right?"

I must have looked stunned, and I was. I slowly leaned back in my lounge chair, searching for words to say, but none came to me. Finally, I sat up, swiveling my chair to see if anyone was around. Once again, Foster looked dead asleep, which was a good thing, because I'd assign him to Davien for the next twenty-four hours while the rest of us slept. Everyone else was settled in the mid-cabin or the aft, possibly resting. "Exactly, *what* has Davien told you?"

"He said last summer, when you all went to the Hamptons for his birthday, you wore some white swimsuit with white netting…"

"Mesh." I corrected him.

"Whatever. He said that you were this 'dark-haired, tan-skinned goddess.'"

My jaw dropped. "He didn't!" *How did I miss this? How long has he liked me?* I wondered. *He CAN'T like me like that!*

"Yup, he did. He admitted that before that, he was really annoyed by your hovering and not letting him fuck around… but after he saw you in that swimsuit, you were it for him."

"What about Halsey?"

"What about her? Senator Nash just wants his daughter to marry someone rich. I'm sure you're aware that the West family will never, *ever* run out of money, even if Davien tries to spend it all." He chuckled at that one, cracked open his other shot and held it out, urging me to get mine ready. When I had, we toasted again before slamming them back. Truth be told, the way this conversation was going, and after the one I'd just had with Adrian... fuck, I could use a fifth of Cuervo instead of these paltry one-hitters.

I settled more comfortably into my chair and looked at my watch; it read a little after one in the morning. "I figure we'll hit Dubai around two, or a little before."

"What time is it?"

"Ten after one. I don't turn my clock forward the ten hours until after we land in Malé."

"Uggh. We need to just get there already!" he lamented and shifted uncomfortably. "Listen, the whole reason he wanted to come here was to spend time with you. I wasn't even part of his plan, but my mom and his dad got this wild idea that he'd have more fun with me tagging along. *Oh yay!* It will be so much fun being the third wheel... but it's not like I could tell them that. Besides, between you and me, we think our parents just want to get it on without Dav or me around."

"Well, that could be, but there's still tons of personnel and security staff at the White House. I just brought my skeleton crew."

As the silence between us grew, I felt the long day's fatigue washing down me from my head to my toes. I plugged my earbuds into the armrest and looked up off-handedly at Connor.

"He told me you smacked him after fucking his mouth with your tongue."

I choked. "He said what?" The incredulity was tangible in my voice. I dropped my earbuds.

"Yeah. He said you were both pretty into it... I mean," he leaned in close, "you weren't at first, but then when you got all into it, well, it wound him up pretty tight." He shifted, looking at Foster, then motioning to me.

I looked over, but Foster was still breathing heavily, his head still slumped to the side, so I relaxed some.

"He said that you grabbed his hair, fucked his mouth, and were into it when he grabbed your ass and ground his dick into you." He choked on the last part.

Serves you right! You shouldn't have heard about this and sure as hell shouldn't be telling me you did.

"Did you kiss him back, or is this another of his bull-shit stories?" he paused, reflecting—studying the horror on my face. "Oh, fuck, it is huh? He always gets me!"

I let him assume Davien had spun a thread and settled into my seat, ready to forget the whole thing.

"I just can't seem to get the details out of my mind," he said more to himself than to me. "I mean, why would he say all those things if..."

I interrupted him, "It doesn't matter, Connor."

"Was he crazy thinking you *were* into it? I mean, he said it felt like you were, that you kissed him back, and that it could've gone further... I mean before you freaked out and smacked him."

"Connor, this is really none of your business, it's not something I feel comfortable discussing with you."

He winked, nodding that he understood, "I'll take that as a *yes*." He stood and walked up to me. "He needs this, ya know. He needs to love someone and feel excited about life again. You could really be good for him." Leaving it at that, he strode from my view.

I tried resting the remainder of the flight to Dubai, during our 6000-gallon refueling spree, and the remaining two hours to Malé, Maldives. It wasn't until I felt warm breath at my ear, and heard "Cori, we're here," that I pried my eyelids open.

Chapter Four

As planned, once we'd swept the property, had settled in and unpacked, I assigned Officer Foster Black to Davien and Connor, while the rest of us got some much-needed shut-eye.

When I opened my eyes, dim moonlight poured into my overwater bungalow. I could see the private pool and chaise lounges out on the deck, and past it, the calm ocean waters. The sky was dark, except for the sliver of moon and bright stars. They were one of the main reasons I enjoyed travelling—to places like Turkey, Iraq, Afghanistan, Fiji, New Zealand, and here, the Maldives— the night sky, or rather, the stars. They never seemed as brightly lit as when I was in dark, wide-open spaces, away from cities, bright lights and bustle. The quieter side of the world knew the night's beauty intimately; it was what us Westerners were missing—at least in my opinion. The inky blackness brought such an intense peace and quiet that it was overwhelming at times. Sometimes, I was merely breathless, but on nights like tonight, I lay mesmerized by the raw beauty.

My eyes adjusted to the dim light and I took a look around the bungalow. Mine was one of the largest. Granted, it was Davien's, but I had an attached room. It was the only way President West would allow Davien to go alone. Adrian was with Connor and I was bunking with Davien.

"Stunning."

I jumped at hearing his voice and fought to see him in the shadows that hugged the corners. There, by the door that adjoined mine to his, he stood still, watching me quietly.

"Where's Foster? What time is it?"

"Around one. You've been out about nine hours."

"Where's Foster?"

"Reading. I went out the living room slider. I told him I wanted to take some 'me time' out on the deck, under the stars."

"And he bought that crap?" I laughed as I pulled myself up, straightening the comforter.

"Why wouldn't he?"

I shrugged. *What am I going to say? Because you've never needed 'you time' since I was hired three years ago? Seriously?*

Davien walked out of the shadows, wearing only his board shorts. I inhaled sharply. He'd most certainly grown up since last summer. His abdomen was etched, an eight-pack clearly defined, and the 'V' disappeared into his low-slung shorts. I noted the strings were laced but not tied. His pecs were cut, and his shoulders and arms ripped. I mean, I'd been to the gym tons of times on security detail for him, but he hadn't looked like this afterward... when *had* he grown into a man? *When did I start seeing him as a man?*

"Swim with me?" The eagerness and hopefulness in his question, caused his voice to hitch. "I mean, we don't have to go in the ocean. The infinity pool would be just as cool."

Against my better judgment, I agreed. "Give me a minute—why don't you go ahead and get in?" He nodded and strode toward the open sliding wall. I dug around in my suitcase until I found my white suit—the same one Connor had mentioned—and headed to the bathroom to put it on.

Satisfied with my loose chignon and the tendrils that cascaded around my face, I hoisted my 'girls' back in place. I gave myself a final once-over before turning off the light and stepping back into the darkness that shrouded my bedroom. I padded softly across the bamboo floor and out the open slider. My feet never made a sound as I closed in on the pool.

"I was wondering if you'd changed your mind." Davien looked up at me and flashed one of his sexy smiles.

Jeezus, I'm so going to regret this later, but I need to get my mind off Adrian. So long as nobody knows, what's the harm in a little dip to relax?

I stepped down the stairs into the pool, its salty warmth enveloping me like a baby floating in its momma's womb. It was so comforting. Any tension I'd felt before entering the water immediately left my weary muscles and wary mind.

"Mmm," I hummed, dipping my shoulders down into the water. "This is heavenly, such a great idea, Davien. Thanks for suggesting it—I wouldn't have gotten in if you hadn't invited me." Flashing him a genuine smile, I headed over to the edge closest to the ocean and rested my forearms in the channel that ran along the entire edge of the pool.

The stars glistened off the top of the waves, light dancing up and down on their crests. I could hear the waves as they rolled in, softly breaking below us against the bungalow's supports.

"Magical, isn't it?"

I startled at the husky voice behind me. Davien glided up. His arm brushed mine as he raised it to hug the side of the pool like I was. Oddly, the simple, accidental touch electrified my skin. *What is wrong with me?* I figured my reaction had more to do with the intimate conversation that I'd had with Adrian earlier than with Davien brushing his arm against mine.

"It's hard to believe we left D.C. almost two days ago already."

"Yeah," I breathed, "the time change nearly accounts for half a day."

"Okay, Ms. Technical," he razzed me and bumped my hip with his own.

"No, I was just saying…" I stopped myself. After all, what was the point? "You know, Dav…" I paused, turning and reaching for his arm. He jumped when my cool hand came to rest on his warm skin. "We don't always have to do this… tension thing."

He cocked his head, his eyes measuring mine, his face pensive and thoughtful. "Do we? I mean, our dynamic, is it always tense?" He chuckled, "Well, maybe there's some tension, I'll give you that… but there's different kinds."

"I don't know. It just always seems like you fight me on everything. I don't want that. I'd rather be your friend than nanny."

"Well then stop… being my nanny, I mean. And before you go off on how Dad hired you and kept you on to take care of me in the absence of my mom, know that while I needed that two or three years ago, I don't need it now. My needs have… changed."

My eyes flickered to his. A blush crept up my neck and spread across my cheeks. "Davien, I run your security detail. It's not practical for me to satisfy your other needs. I'd find myself in need of a job." I laughed and slid my hand from his shoulder, down his muscular arm, before resting it on my other one.

We stared out over the ocean, entranced by the stars' reflections and the gentle lapping of the waves. My body gravitated toward his, and before long, we were hip to hip, shoulder to shoulder.

"Can I ask you something, Cori?" I felt his intense, clear blue eyes measuring me, willing me to look at him. But, in order to do that, I'd be mere inches from his soft, kissable lips, so I continued to stare off toward the ocean's horizon.

"Depends," I prevaricated. "I may not answer if I don't like the question." It was hard not to feel close to him, given as much time as I'd spent with him over the past three years.

"Fair enough." I felt him shift; now his thigh and knee grazed mine. He sighed deeply, as if mustering up courage to ask. "Our kiss, the night before we left…"

Fuck, this again?

He waited, as if hoping I'd jump in and save him from this awkwardness. I maintained my silence. "I mean, it wasn't just me, right? Like, you felt it too, didn't you? I didn't imagine your hands in my hair or your body molding to mine? What happened?"

I turned toward him, just as he ran his fingers through his wet hair. "So, what exactly are you asking me, Dav?"

"Why did you slap me?"

I turned toward him. My arm still rested on the edge of the pool as I gently splashed warm water over my neck and chest. "It really doesn't matter, does it?"

"Yeah, to me it kinda does. I mean, sure, I know you're older than me, and that if we started something, you might lose interest in me, thinking I'm still a fucking kid or whatever, but..."

I interrupted him. "You startled me, okay?" I lowered my voice and looked toward the living room slider. The coast was still clear. "When you kissed me, I fought it. I did." It sounded more like I was trying to convince myself than Davien of this fact. "But my mind and body went numb. I couldn't move." *And I panicked...* I thought back to Iraq and how I never responded under pressure, the way I'd been trained since...

I swallowed. "My body tingled and fired off in all the right places," I sighed, "and all the wrong places. It wasn't something I expected. Kissing you back was not something I was supposed to do." I leaned in toward Davien. "My response to you when you kissed me," I moaned, but went for it, since I was already in this deep, "well, let's just say that I haven't felt that in a *really, REALLY,* long time. So, I slapped you. It was the only way I knew how to regain control of the situation."

Before I could move or put up any resistance, Davien pulled me between him and the tiled wall. His lips met mine with an intensity that stole my breath away and robbed any willpower I had—should I have tried to muster any. His lips seared mine with their heat and ferocity. The kiss was passionately savage and brutal; my lips would feel bruised in the morning.

His teeth grazed my jawline and branded the skin on my neck as he nipped and kissed a hot trail to my shoulder, before returning to my lips, which were slightly parted as I panted with desire. A strong hand drove our kiss, navigating it from my nape, where it had woven in my now loose tresses. His other remained respectful, steering clear of my heaving breasts, but pulling my frame to his with the strong hold he had against my back.

I kissed him with abandon. At first, I'd poured all my pent-up feelings from my earlier dealings with Adrian into this kiss; however, Davien stole every conscious thought from my head once I felt his raging erection against my abdomen. At that moment, it became all about him. *ONLY HIM.*

"Cori," he breathed, "I've wanted this for so long." He nuzzled his mouth into my neck, breathing raggedly into it. I could feel his heart thrumming out of his chest, against the beat of my own.

"This feels so... *wrong*," I admitted warily.

"Not to me," he mumbled into my neck as he held me tightly, his erection noticeably present against my own pulsating intimates.

"I want to, but we just..." I paused, trying to catch my breath, willing my heart and raging hormones to quit their wild assault on my senses, "...can't."

"Damn it, Cori, I want you so bad." Frustration laced his words. "You can't tease me like this and then pretend it means nothing... like last time." His voice hitched in his throat, indicating real emotion lay behind his words.

I rested my forehead on his strong shoulder, "I just don't know…"

Davien pulled back from me, so that the warm salty water now created a barrier between our two energies; two energies that were pulling toward each other, in spite of the moral war I was waging within myself.

"Jeezus, *fuck*," he growled, exasperated. "What is there to know? What more do you need to feel to know that what we'd have, would be fucking amazing?"

"It's not that simple for me. I'm not the president's kid —I don't have an instant get out of jail free card. For me, it's not just about how I feel. I was hired to do a job…"

Davien interrupted me. "Excuses, excuses. Forgive me if it all sounds like bullshit."

"You're nineteen. I wouldn't expect you to understand."

"Low blow playing the age card… Jeezus, Cori. FUCK!"

"Is everything all right out here?"

I looked past Davien and saw Officer Foster Black standing at the lip of the living room slider, eyeing us suspiciously.

"Absolutely! The water's fine. Want to join us?"

"Davien being difficult? Need a break?"

"Nah," I hedged, "he's my charge; it's just a regular day in the office for me."

"Alright, if you say so. Hey, if you've got it, I'd like to get some shuteye?"

"What time is it?"

"Just after 0200."

"Absolutely, Foster. See you back on the clock at 1000?"

"Eight hours." I could hear him sigh from where I was in the pool, even with the waves breaking softly under the bungalow. "If you say so, boss-lady." I could hear the smile in his voice, though, so I wouldn't push the attitude I'd perceived a moment before.

"Call me on your cell. I'll give you your assignment then."

"Roger that."

I watched him turn from the open-wall slider and head inside.

"How's it feel to be the one in charge, never taking orders and always giving them?"

I laughed in disbelief. "*Trust me*," I muttered sarcastically, "I take orders." Before he could ask me from who, I added, "Your *dad*, President Ethan West, has given me strict orders. Why the fuck else do you think I haven't jumped your bones already?"

"I don't know, to be honest, cause with the fucking chemistry we have, it should be a no-brainer... in spite of the fact that my dad's president, or that I'm nineteen. And honestly, it really shouldn't matter if you're head of my security, cause I'd never be safer than when I'd be buried deep inside you.

Holy fuck. This kid, this man, strikes a chord with me. I don't know how much longer I can do this.

Davien closed the gap between us, his warm body so near I could feel him without him actually touching me. He leaned in, his breath hot at my ear, and still, no part of him touched me. My skin was aware, and the small hairs stood on end, just waiting for him to break that invisible barrier between us. "Cori," he hummed, "can't you just imagine how I'd feel sliding into your slick sweetness? How hard I'd be against your velvet softness?"

Where the fuck did you learn to talk like this? Who talks like this? A slight moan escaped from my parted lips, waiting for the kiss I prayed was inevitable.

"I'd worship every inch of your skin, touch all the right spots, even the elusive ones inside you. You'd want for nothing. I'd make you beg for me to make you come and once you did, I'd make you come again and again."

"How did... Where did..." I croaked. "I mean, I've been watching you for the last three years. How did you learn...? God," I groaned. "Never mind. I sound like an idiot."

"At prep-school mostly, during practice, after games, at friends' houses, with friends' mothers, even at the movies. Some of the officers you put in charge... One of them... what was his name, Officer Duggar? He was the easiest, always on his phone and if I said I needed to go do something for fifteen minutes, he let me. No questions asked."

"No shit?" I was glad I'd fired him, but not nearly so glad that I'd changed the subject, because my core still ached, and I still pulsed from the promises he'd made. My lips still silently begged to be kissed. "Hey, Dav, it's getting late. I really need to think about winding this down."

At this, he placed his large palms on my shoulders, sliding them down until he encircled my wrists, cuffing me. He closed the minuscule distance between us, pressing his hard lines into my softer ones. Leaning in, his lips grazed my ear. "Cori..." He lowered himself in the water just enough so my intimates were lined up with his stout erection, which jutted substantially from inside the front of his shorts. "Are you sure," he purred, "I can't change your mind?"

To this, he slid the full length of himself from the entry of my core, all the way until I felt his hardness at my abdomen. His mouth kissed and nipped at my neck. I writhed, struggled to break free from his hold, but there was also something incredibly sexy about being controlled; about NOT being in charge for a change. He took his powerful hips and ground them into me, digging and grinding into my suited intimates until I couldn't take it anymore. "Please," I breathed, "please..." The plea fell from my lips, shameless, hungry and wanton.

Davien released my left hand, which I threw up around his neck and entangled in his waves, crushing my body more fully into his.

"Cori, may I?" he questioned, seeking my permission, which I answered by pulling his mouth down to mine for a deep kiss. His fingers deftly slid my suit aside, palming me fully before entering me with first his index, and then both his index and middle fingers. I am not sure if it was him or me who moaned, but a deep throaty groan came from somewhere deep, somewhere that needed what the other was offering.

I was mad with desire. I no longer felt the wind on my back, or heard the waves breaking. I resided in a world where only he and I existed. That is, until I heard my security phone chiming.

I tore my lips from his, ragged and battle-worn from our intensely passionate endeavor. "I *HAVE* to get that. It's either President West or one of my team." I fought to get my gumby-like body to work for me, but my muscles lacked muscle memory, still drunk from our kiss, and well... my body... *Fuck*. It was all over on that front. My core still fluttered from what he had stirred inside me, and my apex still vibrated—on the verge of finding its release. To put it simply, I was a fucking mess. I fought through the liquid prison that had so recently been my sanctuary, until I reached the stairs. I fumbled climbing them—*Why the fuck won't my body work, damn it?!*

I dashed inside, just as my phone quit ringing. I recognized the number and dialed it in a heartbeat, concerned that there had been a security breech as late as it was. "Adrian, talk to me. Is everything alright?"

"Yes?" He drew out the syllable as though it was weird for me to be asking him that. "Are *you* okay?"

I rolled my eyes, *I would've been more than okay...* "I am but let me get back with you. I just heard something on the other side. Give me ten." I hung up and drew in a deep, cleansing breath. I'd just bought myself ten minutes to compose myself, get my story straight, and get Davien squared away for the night.

I turned back toward the slider and jumped. Davien was standing there. *Goddamn it! Doesn't he know it's dangerous sneaking up on a former soldier like this? Especially one as messed up as me.*

"Guess that means the night's over?" His voice was hopeful, but he'd clearly heard my brief conversation with Adrian.

"It is. Honestly, it should've been when you'd asked me to join you in the pool. I knew what you were really asking and accepted the invitation anyways." I walked up to him and wrapped my chilly arms around his waist. "Thanks for tonight."

"So, what? That's it? You're acting like we're over, like what just happened never took place. What the fuck, Cori?"

I placed my palms on his cheeks, angling his arrogant face down at me so I could look into his striking, clear blue eyes, which looked more like stormy waters than clear seas. "I'm *not* saying that, Davien. What I *am* saying is that right now, at this very moment, I have a job to do. I cannot make you any promises, except one. If I don't call Officer Rogue back when my ten minutes are up, he will be here in a hot second, assuming there's a security breech. What I need is for you to *please*, go to your side and crawl into bed. Watch TV, or act like you're sleeping. It's immaterial, but I need you gone. Now."

He nodded—thankfully getting the message I was sending him—and bent down, brushing a kiss on my forehead before exiting my room through our adjoining doors.

I flew to the slider and pulled the wall panels closed, dragging the heavy blackout curtain across it. Running into the bathroom, I grabbed my thrashed boot camp sweats from my open suitcase. Rushing to put them on, I only paused for a second to look in the mirror. I was flushed. I looked alive. *Maybe Davien is good for me after all...*

I opened the door between my suite and the bungalow and ran to the living room slider. I struggled a bit to get the panels to slide closed, but when I had, the room felt secure. Safe and enclosed. I jogged over to the front door and checked that it had been locked behind Foster. It had been. Lastly, I knocked on Davien's door and quietly opened it. He smiled at me and went back to watching some local TV variety show. I quietly walked back to my room, closing my doors behind me. Grabbing my work phone, I picked it up to text Adrian.

Vette
-False Alarm. All secure here.

Adrian
-9.5 minutes.
On time as usual.

Vette
-Thanks 4 checking in.
I meant 2 earlier.
I'm jet-lagging bad.

Adrian
-Get some rest.
I can cover the morning shift?

Vette
-Nah. It's my job 2 lead my team.
I will just suck it up.

Adrian
-Always the dutiful soldier.
2 tired for a night-cap?

Vette
-It's 0235!

Adrian
-Perfect!
It's Happy Hour back home!

Vette
-IDK Ade...

Adrian
-We have a few things we need 2 address...
That conversation we weren't done having.

Vette
-Waaay 2 tired for that.

Adrian
-2 tired 4 company?
Had U on my mind since the flight.
Would really like 2 C U?

Vette
-Meet me @ the front door.
Don't knock.

> *Adrian*
> -Roger meet you at the front door.
> Don't knock.

I set my phone down beside my bed and shuffled toward my bedroom door. *What have I gotten myself into now?* In less than a minute I was standing on the wooden walkway that led up to my bungalow. I saw Adrian leave his residence and stride toward me. When he reached me, I turned, and he followed me inside. I shut the door, and we walked in silence to my room.

I closed the door and headed for my bed. "I warned you I was tired, but you wanted to talk. So, talk, on my terms." I smiled at him pleasantly, climbing under the covers, still in my thrashed boot camp sweats.

"I'm sure I don't need to ask, but who's watching Connor?"

"I called Officer Cruz. He wasn't any too happy I was waking him up, but I spun a thread about how you needed me to go over tomorrow's deets. Anthony's already messaged me that he's posted there." He smiled as he rounded my side of the bed. "No worries. It's *all* taken care of."

"Well, kick your shoes off and climb in then." I patted the bed beside me, encouraging my best friend to take a load off. "So, what did you want to *discuss* exactly?" I jested. "Cause if it's a lecture, you can walk your silly ass back out my door."

Adrian did exactly as I'd encouraged him to do and settled in. He snuggled up next to me and wrapped his muscular arm around me.

He and Davien were such polar opposites. Where Davien was *mostly* proper and groomed for politics, Adrian couldn't care less about propriety and decorum, and you sure as hell wouldn't see him running for any type of political position. Davien was obviously younger, and with it, he lacked maturity—or call it life experience. In contrast, Adrian was hewn from the cloth of life. He was mature, responsible and the most dependable person I knew. I could count on him with my life, and his past experiences were reflected in how he handled all situations with ease. I guess, after being shot at, the rest of the shit life threw at him must have seemed pretty easy to take. I know similar experiences have forever changed me.

The men were close to the same size, but I'd never felt as secure and protected as when I was in Adrian's arms. He was ripped, muscular and fit. Not one of those sausage-beefcakes you see pumping iron at the gym, although I'm sure his Adonis-like physique wasn't just from rock climbing, hiking, biking and all the other sports he did.

Davien's body though, was just that—sure, he swam, and his shoulders showed it, but the rest... well, that was from hours in the gym. He was lean and fit too, but somehow, his frame lacked the strength Adrian's had. Not that I was complaining about either—fuck, what kind of girl would I be if I did? It's just, Davien was somehow... softer. *It's because he doesn't have 'killing' eyes... the eyes of a war-torn soldier who's taken lives. Much, unfortunately, like my own.* I sighed heavily.

"Where's your head at, Vee?" He squeezed me for good measure.

"I don't know, just thinking about stuff."

He chuckled, "Shit, when aren't you?"

I looked up at his warm, chestnut eyes, and butterflies exploded in my gut. *Fuck.* "Life's just crazy, right? I mean like with us. Who would've ever thought that after our past in Iraq..." I exhaled.

"Vee, I'd rather leave that chapter buried."

Instantly, my bodied hardened against his side. "Sure, fine. Whatever." I sat up and tried to find more space between our bodies. "Why did you want to come over so badly, Ade? I'm tired, and moody, jet lagging badly... I thought you wanted to talk about our conversation on the plane?"

"I'm concerned about you getting entangled in President West's web."

"Oh?" This sounded interesting.

"Connor's been talking my goddamn ear off; you know, he wants you and the *kid* together. I think he's hoping that if Ethan is fixated on the affair between you two, then he won't be as focused on his mom... at least that's what I've gathered."

"How would Ethan find out? There'd be no way the president would know unless... *oh...*," It hit me with the force of a head-on collision. "Connor is going to say something."

"It sounds that way, Vee. Like I said earlier, if you get blacklisted by the president, you aren't working for anyone in D.C." He pulled me in tighter to him. "I don't know what it is," he breathed softly, "but being this close to you has always made me feel—*centered*. At home." He shook his head, as though to snap out of the spell I was unknowingly spinning. "Anyways," he cleared his throat, "I just think you really need to be careful when it comes to Davien. He comes with a whole boatload of bullshit, and suppose you guys hit it off, where would it go? What future do you see with him?"

I shrugged. "I haven't gotten that far."

"You!?" His shock registered in his voice. "The girl who overthinks everything? Besides, remember Tanner Lyons? My second in Iraq? He's been pestering the shit out of me to put a bug in your ear. He wants in."

I laughed, still shaken by Adrian's earlier confession. *Somewhere in that big head of his, I still do it for him!* "Oh yeah, great. That's the last thing I need, hooking up with your guy best friend. Then we'd be locked into a weird triangle forever."

"Triangle?" And then it dawned on him, as if he didn't already know. "Vee, I'm seeing Natalie."

"I know, but it isn't serious; at least, I didn't think it was."

"Well, it's not, but you and I work together every day."

"So? I'd be working every day with Tanner, too."

He squeezed me, "You've got me there." He sighed. "It's just, I don't know, I thought we'd moved on to being *just* friends."

I looked up at him, searching his warm, honey depths for any sign of encouragement.

"Fuck, Vee," he grated. "Your damn eyes... your goddamn green eyes still do it for me."

His mouth collided with mine, as though we were two magnets who'd been instantly flipped, our attractions now pulled toward the other instead of pushing. His tongue ran across my lips, and I parted them, inviting him in. He aggressively sought mine, and we engaged in a match; spearing and jousting, nipping and biting. Instantly, I grew wet with need, a need that had been long denied, a thirst that only Adrian could quench.

With the skill of a lover who knows what he's doing, he slid his hand off my shoulder to my hip. He seized the other and spun me effortlessly onto his lap, so that I straddled him. His large, strong hands gripped my hips possessively. Memories of our nights together in Iraq flooded back to me as I felt his engorged erection at my clothed apex.

His left hand clenched my loose tresses as his right grasped my hip tighter, guiding it in a salacious dance. He rocked me back and forward as he thrust, his movements restrained, but did nothing to disguise the passion that had been belayed for far too long.

"Jeezus, Ade..." I struggled for the words to convey what this meant, how good this felt. "God, I've wanted this for..."

"...ever." He rasped, finishing my sentence through clenched teeth.

I could only nod as my mouth danced with his, my emotions too tumultuous to express. His hand went from being entangled in my hair, to tenderly touching my face, and then back to my nape, guiding the cadence of our kiss. Our passion was all over the board, first fervent and needy, then passionate, then soft and tender, and last... back to lustful and shameless. His hand on my hip elicited more moans from me as he rocked me on his erection. Our clothes did nothing to hide our need, or my readiness for him.

Then, as suddenly as our licentious affair began, it ended. His hand slid from my hair, to my shoulder, and from my hip, to rest quietly on my thigh. He pulled back, abandoning my lips. The sound of our labored breaths echoed off the walls of my room.

"Damn it," Adrian grumbled as he lifted me off his lap, simultaneously shifting out of my way. He rolled off the opposite side of my bed and adjusted himself.

"Ade? Adrian?"

"Give me a minute," he grumbled.

It stung. *How can he be so cold now, so emotionally vacant? Did I do something wrong?* I slid off the bed, grabbed a pair of leggings and took them to the bathroom to change.

When I came out, I noticed my curtains had been opened and soft, incandescent light streamed in through the closed slider. Adrian stood there, pensive, looking out at the black ocean. He must have sensed I was there, because without even looking at me he began to talk, in a pained voice, "I'm sorry, Vee."

I walked up to him, placing my hand tenderly on his shoulder. He stiffened, so I let it slide off.

"You're my superior; it was unprofessional that I took the liberties that I did…"

I cut him off angrily, "Is that what this is about? Cause I don't give a damn about being your boss right now." I moved toward the slider, turning so I could see his face. I looked him in the eyes. "What is going on? Did I do something wrong? Why are you always shutting me out?"

Adrian looked down at me, his chestnut eyes lacking their usual luster and zest for life. "I thought I'd moved past this. Sorry."

"Will you quit apologizing? What's really going on?"

He stood there for a time, cold as steel. I decided it was best not to push him. I could see it was more of the same, more of Iraq, and I didn't want to go months this time without my best friend. Work would be awkward, and the last thing I wanted was for him to put in for a transfer.

Finally, he slapped his palms on the glass, resting them there as he leaned his forehead between them. He shook his head sadly. "I can't. I just can't do this with you."

"Adrian?" I reached for him, but my hand fell short. "Ade, I don't understand. Don't do this again. Please, at least give me something, some reason why..." my voice quivered, constricted by the confusion, fear and so many more emotions balled up inside me. Silent tears travelled down my face.

"Vee, it's nothing personal." I opened my mouth to protest, but he continued. "It's me. We're just not good for each other." At that quiet disclosure, he pushed away from the slider and headed toward my bedroom door.

"The hell we're not!" I snarled, pissed.

"Vee, I'm not... you're not going to do this. I'm seeing Natalie. Maybe it works out for us and maybe not, but I'm not being fair to her. You also need to consider Davien's feelings in all of this."

"What about being fair to me, or don't I count?"

He sighed heavily. "Of course you count, but I don't want to ruin what you and I have. You're my best friend, and I don't want to lose that."

"What makes you think this won't work?"

"Trust me, I know me. With you, I'm not myself. I feel too..." he sighed, his composure wavering a brief moment before the walls slammed back up. "Trust me, it just won't." He headed with finality toward my door, "I'll let myself out." His words were icy, cold, unfeeling. He opened my door. "See you tomorrow."

That was it. He walked away from me. The sound of the door clicking was like a knife to my heart. A million thoughts ran through my mind but one stood out—*he hates the vulnerability I bring out in him.*

The soft rap on my door cleared that realization from my mind.

"Not now." My voice sounded harsh, even to me. I ran my fingers through my hair and strode to the patio slider, resting my forehead on the cold glass and closed my eyes. Images of Adrian, of our future and kids, fought their way in as I sadly watched the silent movie play-out in my head. Unwanted, salty tears slid from my eyes, burning my sunburned and wind-chaffed cheeks.

"Cori?"

I jumped at Davien's voice, but did nothing to acknowledge him. I was too embarrassed to face him.

I felt his body behind mine, and surprisingly welcomed the warmth of his arms as they slid around my waist. He gently turned me, cradling my head to his hard chest, rubbing my back comfortingly.

"Want to talk?"

I could only shake my head no, for fear sobs would win over if I tried to say anything.

"I couldn't help but over-hear... you two have a past." I felt him shake his head against the top of my own.

"Officer Rogue's a fool if he can't see what an amazing woman you are."

A choked sob escaped from my parted lips. "Why?" I questioned pitifully. "I don't understand why he's such a bullheaded man! Adrian insists we aren't right for one another." I wiped the tears from my eyes, and from Davien's chest, putting some room between our bodies. "This isn't the first time he's done this to me."

"I don't get it, Cori." Davien's voice cracked. "Why do you want someone who doesn't want you and doesn't see your worth, when I'm right here? I'm right here and know how amazing you are, and how great we'd be together. Why won't you just give me a try... give us a fair shot?"

I reached up, tenderly touching his cheek.

"Is it the age thing... cause damn it, Cori, there's not a damn thing I can do about being fifteen years younger than you." He chuckled and smiled arrogantly, "I can't say that I lack any experience in that department though." He winked salaciously. "I *know* I can satisfy you."

I gave him a playful smack on the cheek. "Davien, it's not that. Not the age thing *entirely*... I just feel, well, I feel I'd be betraying Kait and Ethan's trust. And then too, there's how unfair it is to start something with you when I can't give you my whole self. I mean, you know I'm all fucked up." I wrapped my arms around myself. "And let's not forget, this is my JOB. It's entirely possible I won't have one once Connor blabs his mouth off to your father."

Davien stepped toward me, closing the distance between us that I had created. He slid his strong arm around my waist and tilted my chin up with the other, so that I was looking into his soulful eyes. He lowered his head, grazing first my forehead, then my lips with his own. "Cori, I like you. Like—I *really* like you—and all my dad wants for me is to be happy. He knows how hard it was for me when mom died." He grazed my lips gently again, as though he were tracing them with his. "He'll get over it. If you have any feelings for me at all, do this. Be with me, cause I guaran-fucking-tee you won't regret it."

At that, his lips lowered to mine in a languorous, seeking kiss. My toes curled, my core fluttered, and I gave myself over completely to him at that instant.

Chapter Five

I settled into the couch at the aft of the cabin with my fountain pen and journal—*I guess I'd better do as the good doctor prescribed and get some of this shit out of my head.* The pen began to glide effortlessly across the page...

If it hadn't been for Davien, I never would've made it through this past week. Thankfully, though, he and I have grown closer. It eased the pain of losing Adrian... again.

I wiped angrily at a single renegade tear.

After Adrian left my room that first night, Davien came in and found me crying. He'd comforted me, then seduced me, and I'd let him.

"You two have a past." It wasn't a question. It was as though he'd understood the pain I was in and decided not to be an ass about it. He matured in my eyes and gained my respect. He'd made me forget about Adrian for the night through kisses and quiet laughter, and had nursed me through the next couple of days.

Adrian and I? Well, fuck. Where to start?

We just went back to as normal as possible. He acted like nothing happened, and I've tried my damnedest to keep it professional. I've done pretty well, I think.

So far today, we all had lunch on the beach, splashed in the clear waters the Maldives are famous for, and even swam with stingrays and turtles. It's been a good day.

Adrian joined Davien and me in our motorcade to the airport earlier, and even that went off without a hitch. We all visited and joked with each other. It appeared as though Adrian and I were back to being best friends again, which to Davien's credit, he's been handling like a pro.

I felt a light touch on my shoulder and looked up from my journaling, into a hypnotizing set of clear blue eyes that were quickly becoming my favorite. Davien motioned for me to remove my earplugs. "What's up?" I said sunnily, flashing him a big, genuine smile. I'd found that so long as I wasn't around Adrian, being happy was relatively easy; otherwise, it was a chore.

"The captain just announced we need to prepare for landing." He offered his hand to me, which I gladly accepted. He pulled me up from the clutches of the couch I'd been lying on for the past hour or so, while writing about the past week.

We walked from the rear of the plane, through the mid-cabin, to the café-lounge seats in the front cabin. I nodded to Adrian and Foster before taking the seat

Davien—ever the gentleman—had swiveled for me. Adrian would've just plopped down across from me. Like I'd noted on fifty if not a hundred occasions, these two men were polar opposites. Davien buckled into the leather seat across the teak table from me, and without pause, took my hand in his. Reality seeped in that we needed to reprise our roles, and I pulled mine out from under his.

Chapter Six

Sliding into a seat across from a stern, all business President Ethan West, I watched as he signed a document that his assistant had brought him. "Thank you, Ollie. That will be all for now."

Ollie nodded politely at his dismissal. I followed him with my eyes as he strode confidently from the Oval Office. My gaze returned to the president. He sat there, his hands clasped, studying me. I felt my back straighten as I subconsciously squared up my shoulders.

"Officer Renyols?" He paused for effect.

I waited for him to say something else, but he just sat there glowering at me. His scowl unnerved me. "Sir?" I prodded as I fought to keep panic under lock and key.

"I'm sure you have surmised why I have called you in here." He dropped his clasped hands onto a manila folder that lay on his desk. He opened it and removed a document, which he began to read from.

"Officer Vette Renyols, when you were asked if you have engaged in vaginal/penal sexual intercourse with my son; you answered no. The test confirmed that was the truth. When you were asked if you had engaged in any form of anal penetration; you answered no. The test confirmed that was the truth. When you were asked if you had engaged in cunnilingus, you answered no. The test confirmed that was the truth. When you were asked if you had engaged in fellatio, you answered yes. The test confirmed that was the truth. When asked if my son had placed objects; fingers, vibrators, phallic toys inside your vagina; you answered yes. The test confirmed that was the truth." He closed the folder, clearing his throat uncomfortably. "Do I need to continue?"

I struggled to hear him past the loud beating of my heart, and shallow breaths I fought to suck in. "No, sir."

"I'm sorry, but I didn't hear you." His eyes remained steely and fixed squarely on me. I squirmed under his intense scrutiny, my clammy hands tightly folded over the chair armrests.

I cleared my throat and hedging my trembling, I held onto what little self-respect I had left, "No. Sir."

"So, then... after reviewing the lie-detector results, I have determined that you were being forthcoming and honest with me earlier when I had questioned you about the nature of yours and Davien's relations." At this, his gaze softened a hair as he leaned back in his chair. "I am not in the habit of apologizing, but I'm doing exactly that. It was wrong of me to accuse you of lying." He sighed. "Vette, can I just talk to you as a father to his... his son's girlfriend?"

My eyes grew wide, as I gently shook my head from side to side in disbelief, some of my panic subsiding. "Yes, Mr. President. I would like that very much."

"Well, then call me Ethan."

"Sir... err, Ethan." My heart still beat erratically.

"Vette, Kait and I welcomed you into our home over three years ago when my son was a strapping sixteen-year-old in love with his high school sweetheart, Amity. We took a risk on you. Your personnel file was strong. You'd proven yourself in your military career, and again while working for Academi. Your references were glowing and your conduct impeccable. You received the highest level of security clearance and have maintained it through the duration of your career... I mean, we took all of these things into account."

He leaned forward, placing his elbows on his mahogany desk. "The one thing that gave me pause—the bombing and terrorist incident in Iraq— Kait glossed over, commenting that many contributing members of society had PTSD and pasts they could not escape from, and who were we to deny you your history for a future with us?" His eyes moistened, and his voice grew suddenly soft. His gentleness did nothing to prevent the terrible memories from welling up, restarting my panicked pulse. *Iraq. That fateful day. The terrorist. The gunfire. The explosion. The pain...*

"Kait adored you from the get-go and was convinced that having you in Davien's life was the right move. She wanted you to give Amity a run for her money, be there for Dav when she wasn't... It was as though she looked right into the future and had this all mapped out."

"Sir." I cleared my throat, trying to speak through my frozen vocal cords. "I NEVER had *any* intention of this happening."

"Well, that's good because *THIS* isn't going to happen. Your relations with Davien ended the moment you walked into this room. Is that clear?"

My heart shuddered as it slammed shut, denying me the freedom to decide what was in my best interest. I'd known this was coming, but it didn't make the finality of it all any easier. I willed away tears, but they welled up in spite of my efforts to keep them at bay. "Yes, Mr. President. Crystal," I croaked. I hadn't admitted it, but Davien had made me forget Adrian, even if just for a brief time... and I'd been happy these past few weeks.

"Exactly how did it happen, if you don't mind me asking?"

"Of course." I took a deep breath, willing, praying my nerves and panic response would just *fucking* stop. "I entered his apartment one night at his request to go out... if memory serves it was nearing 0300. Davien had been drinking and came on to me. I shut that down immediately, but it planted a seed, which grew under all of his flirtatious attentions toward me on his birthday trip. He knows what he wants and makes sure he gets it."

A genuine smile of pride spread across the president's

face, "I'll be damned. I'd wondered—just between you and me—that's how I finally got my Kait." He chuckled softly. "I guess the apple doesn't fall far from the tree."

"No, Mr. President, it would appear that it doesn't."

"Ethan."

"Ethan, I recognize my gross lapse in judgement, taking your trust for granted. For that I am gravely sorry."

President Ethan West sat back up, straight in his chair, resuming his role as Head of State. "Yes, well, trust is a curious thing. As it turns out, you've redeemed yourself by being so honest, which is why I am not going to blacklist you in D.C. or fire you; however, you will not be head of Davien's security anymore."

I nodded as I drew in a shaky breath, "I understand, Sir."

He buzzed Ollie and the door immediately opened. "Take Officer Renyols and debrief her on the opportunities I am affording her."

"Yes, Mr. President."

I rose, nodding to Ethan, and followed Ollie from the Oval Office as three men in suits came in at that same time.

I glanced at my watch, 0137. I walked through the empty corridors of the executive quarters, closing doors and turning off lights. I walked past my room, pausing in front of Davien's. I hesitated before knocking. He needed his sleep since he was scheduled to fly out today in a few hours, but the desire to say goodbye on my own terms encouraged me to rap softly on his door.

We've grown so close these past few weeks since getting home from his birthday trip. I wonder how he's going to take this news?

I struggled to calm my pounding heart. The surge of adrenaline from my earlier confrontation with the president made me uncomfortable as it brought back the same bodily responses from that fateful day. I leaned against the door, my breathing shallow, panic threatening to consume me.

The door creaked softly on its hinges as Davien cracked it, then held it wider for me to slip in. He embraced me before the door clicked in its jamb. I collapsed into his arms.

"Jeezus, Cori. Are you okay?" His tone was concerned, and he held me tightly as he stroked my hair. I just trembled in his arms, my façade down, vulnerable. "Man, Cori, I've missed you. Please, tell me you're okay. Is everything alright? What's wrong?"

I nuzzled into his chest. He smelled of sandalwood and spicy vanilla. It wouldn't work on everyone, but Davien smelled good; a little spicy and sweet. It was a heady concoction when mixed with his pheromones, and I swam in his scent. He held me tightly. His hand held my head to his chest as he laid kisses on my crown, the other drew me tightly to his hard body.

"Are you going to miss this place? I know I am," he mumbled softly against my head. "I can't wait until it's just you and me up at Columbia."

I squeezed him around his trim waist, then glided my clammy, trembling hands up his chest to his neck, pulling his lips down to mine. I grazed his soft, full ones, gently kissing him, waiting for my invitation to be accepted. When he parted his lips, I slid my tongue into his eager mouth. Shudders rippled through me as soon as our tongues touched. My mouth coupled with his, as his tenderly caressed mine. He trailed kisses along my jawline, to my neck, sending another shockwave coursing through my body.

"Mmm, you like that, don't you?" he growled huskily, his voice laden with pent up passion. He backed me against the wainscoted wall. Like the first time we'd kissed, he hitched my leg up over his hip. His arousal pressed against my intimate places. He kissed me deeply, his ardor becoming more fervent and eager. I responded to his enthusiastic kiss with as much passion and welcomed his tempestuous touches as they became more demanding against my ass. His hand slid from my rear, up my abdomen, dropping my leg. He found my bra clasp and released my breast into his strong hand, while his other went to work fumbling with the button on the front of my jeans.

I shook my head, willing myself to clear the intoxication from my senses. "Davien, wait," I whispered against his lips. "Wait. Not like this. We can't."

His hands froze their pursuit, and he brought them up to my face, holding it endearingly. "You're right. We've waited this long; you deserve a bed." He laughed throatily, his tenor edged with heavy lust and mischievousness.

"No, I mean... we *can't*."

His sparkling, clear blue eyes met mine with an iciness that surprised me.

"Of course not," he grumbled under his breath, as he went to work adjusting his belt buckle and hard erection in his jeans.

I reattached my bra and straightened my shirt, hanging my head guiltily. *Davien deserves better than me. I shouldn't have let it get this far; not tonight, not ever.*

"Davien," I breathed, still fighting my thrumming heart and the lusty hormones flowing rampant in me, "this isn't easy for me, either." I looked up at him, reaching for his hand. "Please, let's talk?"

He begrudgingly took the hand I offered and followed me to his leather couch. I sat down, facing him, and placed my hand on his knee, as much for his benefit as mine. I hoped it would still my nerves.

"The President," I began nervously, "I mean Ethan... err, your dad called me into the Oval Office today."

"Shit." He and I both knew that being called in there was a big deal.

"Yes, you could say that." I took in a deep, cleansing breath to steady my nerves. "He said it had come to his attention recently that you and I have entered into a 'less than appropriate' relationship." I ran my fingers through my long black hair. "Dav, he's sending you to Columbia without me." I watched Davien, as his whole demeanor crumpled.

I squeezed Davien's thigh. "He asked me how far it's gone. I had to tell him, Dav. He said, based on his intel, that I was lying. Can you believe he had me take a lie detector test?" A slight sob escaped past my lips. "It was so degrading. He had *his* head security officer, Daniel Cook, hook me up and conduct the test." I shivered from the uncomfortable memory. "He asked me intimate details, Dav... even went through a list of items and body parts that you may have *put* in me."

Davien's leg jounced with nervous, angry energy and he wrung his hands. "Goddamn it!" he said, slamming his fist onto the armrest. "He has no right! So what if he's the fucking president; he's not God."

I sobbed again at his outburst. The last thing I'd wanted was to come between them. My pulse was racing, and familiar panic was beginning to take its stronghold.

Davien pulled me into his warm embrace. "Sorry, Cori. Dad can be a real asshole, but really, what can I do about it? Image and all. I can't ruin his career..."

It was suddenly all so clear how right Adrian had been. How wrong I'd been. I'd been enjoying the attentions of my charge to drown out the pain my best friend had caused. He'd called it exactly, how this would all play out, and that there was no future between Davien and myself.

I knew there was no future between Dav and I deep down; I'd just wanted to prove Adrian wrong for the sake of being right. I hate that he knew Davien and I had no future... uncanny how he'd said the same thing about him and me. I shook my head at the striking parallels.

"Well, thankfully we haven't had intercourse." I shook my head. "My conversation with your dad could've gone a lot worse... Adrian told me this would happen."

"Fuck Adrian. What's Dad's plan for you?"

I pulled back and wiped the tears from my cheeks. "He's considering a possible new position for me, but I may request a transfer from the Executive Residence to the grounds... or I may accept an offer from the private military company Constellis, who acquired Academi." I sighed. "I owe a lot to Academi, and it's why the CIA even looked at my resume for this position." I fidgeted uneasily. "I received a call from Lucas Maxwell of Constellis today, and there's a few openings..."

He interrupted. "Let me guess, for you and *Adrian*." It was a sarcastic statement, which he didn't even bother to disguise as a question.

"And Tanner Lyons," I added. "He's recruiting us because we all served together in Iraq. I have the intelligence analysis and paramilitary skills he's looking for, and of course, they're all military trained special ops guys."

"Of course," he said flatly. "So then, who's heading up security at Columbia, or don't I matter to him anymore?"

I drew in a slow breath. "Senator Powell's team. Amity is back from her senior year in Italy and has decided to pursue a degree there in the performing arts." I hurried on about Davien's first crush. "From what I've heard, she's quite an artful dancer."

"Ami's going to be there?" I could hear shock in his voice. He'd shared that he'd lost his virginity to Amity when they were fifteen and had dated right up to when Kait had passed away. Her last request of her son, as he told it, was to find a *better*, more virtuous girl than his love for the past three years. So, Amity had left the state, and eventually the country, heading to Italy with her older brother for school... and ultimately a break from Davien.

I stood up and pulled him to me, embracing him as a friend now. "See," I spoke softly into his chest, "this could be a good thing. You've shared how deeply you cared for her, and I suspect, if you give it a chance, those feelings you still carry could be rekindled."

"I'm so fucking tired of Dad controlling me." I could hear the anger in his voice. "I've fucking had it, Cori." He broke our embrace and stormed toward his closet like a tornado. I watched as he pulled out his backpack and threw some clothes and necessities into it.

As he approached me, I could see that red had crept

up his cheeks and tears streamed down them. He threw his pack down on the couch and reached out for me. I allowed myself to be pulled into his arms. He squeezed me and, looking down at me with his sparkling blue eyes, planted a soft, endearing kiss on my forehead. "I'm gonna miss the hell out of ya, Cori. You're an amazing woman and you've taught me a lot in the past few weeks. I feel like I've grown up so much, just so I could keep up with you."

"You've matured a lot, Dav."

"Well, I had to, to try to prove I was worth your time," he kidded. "But I'm definitely going to miss the way you smell, and those jade green eyes of yours and..." he added jokingly, "that *fucking* sexy as all hell white swimsuit of yours. The one with mesh sides."

"The netting?" I ribbed him back and flashed him a big smile... referencing one of our inside jokes. "Mmm, I'm sure going to miss you, Davien," I admitted, squeezing him one final time. "Thanks for being everything I needed when I had no one."

I gazed up at him. Our eyes connected, his expression mixed with anger toward his dad and excitement at the possibilities of a future away from here, away from the controlling heavy hand of his father, and mine stormy, my future undecided. He placed his hand on the small of my back and walked me to the door, opening it for me. I stepped into the hall.

"Hey, you've got this. If anyone can recover from Dad's

bullying, it's you. Who knows; maybe something can happen now with you and *Officer* Adrian Rogue?"

Yeah, maybe something can... if he can ever get over his damned, misplaced nobility and superior attitude.

I shrugged and smiled. "Bye, Davien." Squeezing him one last time, I found it hard to walk away. I looked back up to his eyes. "You've got this. I'm really proud of you for standing up for what you believe and demanding the freedom to live your life your way. You'd better take care of yourself. Don't get caught leaving by your dad's security staff, and keep me updated. I can only give you a sixty-minute head start before I need to report you're missing." I confided, as I released him.

"I will, I promise... bye, Cori."

"Bye."

The door closed with heavy finality, just like this chapter of my life...

-THE END-

ALSO BY TINA MAURINE

Look for: Volition

A Uniform & Lace Romance

Book One of Noah & Tessa's Story

Look for: Tina Maurine's story in: Kissing Midnight

A New year's Crazy Ink Anthology

Look for: Tina Maurine's story in: Just Love

A Crazy Ink Anthology

Look for: Tina Maurine's story in: Hushed Affairs

A Forbidden Romance Anthology by Wild Dreams Publishing

Coming soon: Vexed

A Uniform & Lace Romance

A Novella in Noah & Tessa's Story

Coming soon: Veneration

A Uniform & Lace Romance

Book Two of Noah & Tessa's Story

ACKNOWLEDGMENTS

First I want to thank God for instilling my love of writing and for giving me the gift of expression through writing. There were many times I wondered if I were on the right path, but I always came back to Him and when I did I became refocused and confident in my choices. Writing centers me and genuinely makes me happy.

I need to thank Mary, because without her... this this story would never have been written, the Political Romance Anthology that this story originally appeared in, wouldn't have happened, it was her brain-child. Thanks too for your constant support! I can't wait for our third anthology!

To my team—my friends—who I trust and depend on: Jude, Simone, Kristi, Mary, Bec, Bella, YM, Katie...

~THANK YOU~

Without you, Impasse would've never reached its full potential. Thanks for your TIME! Your edits, feedback, honesty and criticisms. You all make me a better writer.
XOXO

Lastly, to my friends and family. For without your love and understanding, I'd never have the confidence, or feel I have the time to pursue my dream. Writing makes me whole, and I appreciate and love you all for understanding this about me.

EXCERPT

Excerpt

Volition
A Uniform & Lace Romance
Noah & Tessa's Story
~Book One~

All Rights are Reserved and Copyrighted
2018 by Tina Maurine
(Excerpt shortened from final publication.)

Ari walked up with drinks for the three of us. He sat down on the shore with his. I took mine, leaned back on my elbows and closed my eyes, taking a long drink.

"Perfect," I purred. "Thank you, Ari. It's just what I needed... a drink to get over my hangover." I smiled at him sincerely and winked before dreamily closing my eyes. Even holding my glass, and with my elbows in the soft silica mud, my legs floated effortlessly on top of the hot mineral water. No trace of my headache lingered.

"So, baby girl, did you ever figure out who Noah Garren and Dirk Archibladt were?"

I peeked at him under hooded eyes as he jounced his eyebrows playfully up and down.

"Dirk, no, but there's something about Noah..."

"Are you effin' kidding me?" Sam shot me a look like I was slow as I moved back away from the group a bit into even shallower water. I didn't want to have to worry about getting the seawater in my drink as I half reclined with one elbow in the mud, my legs floating out in front of me. I closed my eyes, cogitating on her snide comment and judgmental look, but they did nothing to my mood—I was healing from my hangover—as I absorbed the heat, steam, mud, my elixir... everything. I wasn't going to let her ruin my good mood. It had taken me all morning to get it.

A strong hand glided up my left calf. My eyes flew open and Mr. Familiar-For-Some-Reason Noah sprawled on his elbows in the mud floating beside me. He smiled, and I noticed how straight and pretty his white teeth were; a good sign that he didn't chew or smoke. He walked himself up on his elbows until he reached shoulder to shoulder with me. I took my time *once again* admiring his tanned, rugged good looks, thick hair, strong shoulders and back, nice firm ass and killer legs. His legs extended a good ten to twelve inches or so past mine, so he was about a foot taller than me, easily over six feet. I'd have to see him standing to be sure.

He smiled a shit-eating grin at my blatant perusal, before turning over onto his back. As my gaze combed back up his body, I noticed his strong thighs, taut six-pack, and an amazing chest that had a hint of ink hiding under the silica mud that covered most of his body. His chuckle brought me back from my lollipop walk down his yummy body.

"Like what you see?" Noah gave me a notably arrogant smirk. Then it dawned on me... his voice. It was the same husky baritone that had whispered in my ear last night after the last dance. Those amazing hands had been on my hips. The real kicker though—those full, sensual lips and already nipped at my neck. My nipples grew hard at the thought. Now, it was my turn to blush.

What were the fucking chances Ari would invite him? A million to one? How could he know? He wasn't even at the club. If he had known, would he have invited him?

"I could ask you the same thing," I countered back flirtatiously, successfully playing off an arrogant indifference just for the fun of it.

"I knew you'd look good, but had no idea... I mean, damn." His honest admission caused crimson to creep across his cheeks and ears in a blush I wouldn't have expected from this hunk of a man. He was, after all, security, and many of them had been Special Ops or skilled Artillerymen who had seen action on previous tours, and *I* had made *him* blush. It brought a genuine smile of victory to my lips.

"You never did answer me," he prodded back.

"Well shit, Noah—what do you think?" With that, I arched my back, dipping my hair in the water and thrusting my chest into the air. I closed my eyes and inhaled deeply. *God, the water feels amazing.* Its heat eased the tension in my achy, hung-over muscles and felt luxurious as it gently swathed my throbbing head. *Right now, there's no place I'd rather be. I'm so glad I came. I'll have to make sure to thank Ari for such an incredible hangover cure.*

I felt Noah's confidence radiating from every pore in his body; our chemistry undeniable, mutual sexual tension so thick you could cut it. He sidled up, saucily— hip to hip with me and turned on his side, his package firm against my hip, and draped his forearm across my taut abs. His hand rested on my hip farthest from him as his fingers gripped me in a possessive gesture. "Maybe you'll give me the chance to take you out on a real date?"

I opened my eyes and saw intense, hopeful ones looking back at me.

ABOUT THE AUTHOR

Tina Maurine is the gal on the sidelines at the party. The gal who smiles at everyone, but rarely initiates conversation; never the center of attention, but always taking notes on those who are. She loves watching people, their authentic responses to everyday occurrences and in turn has turned years of notes into fodder for her stories, an encyclopedia of emotions and character traits that come alive on the page. She never feels more alive than when she is creating; be it stories, music, graphic art, or painting rocks and canvases with her daughter.

She is a wife, mom, best friend, secretary, teacher, cheerleader, house-straightener, chef, chauffer, video game playing, Barbie doll dressing domestic multi-tasker. She likes her French baguettes crispy, her beer dark, and her chocolate even darker. Her music tastes are eclectic, but if there's a beat, you can bet her body is moving to it... even in the car... and the louder the better.

Tina Maurine lives in Oregon with her amazing husband of twelve years, and their two beautiful children. Prior to marriage and children, she served eight years in the United States Navy and saw the world. She and her husband share their love for travel with their kids, and take as many family trips as their busy schedules allow. When they aren't hitting the road or the skies, and when she isn't teaching, Tina is content to sit at the table in their backyard with her keyboard or a good, sexy book, and watch the kiddos play.

Follow her on Twitter and Instagram @
TinaMaurineAuth

Email: tinamaurine@hotmail.com

http://facebook.com/tina.maurine.1

http://tinamaurine.com

Trient Press

3375 S Rainbow Blvd

#81710, SMB 13135

Las Vegas,NV 89180

Ordering Information:
Quantity sales. Special discounts are available on quantity purchases
by corporations, associations, and others. For details, contact the
publisher at the address above.
Orders by U.S. trade bookstores and wholesalers. Please contact Trient
Press: Tel: (775) 996-3844;   or visit www.trientpress.com.

Printed in the United States of America

Publisher's Cataloging-in-Publication data
Maurine, Tina.
A title of a book : Impasse
ISBN

     Paperback   978-1-953975-22-5
     E-book   978-1-953975-23-2

"Hello everyone," said the human, having recovered her stability. "I'm Lula Pinnock, one of the Earth Languages Translators at Unity. We'll be meeting every Tuesday and Thursday at 19:00. Thursday is two evenings from tonight. Vert has asked me to lead this group and help you learn more about my planet's cultures."

The human glanced at Vert, the Camassan. He dipped his central frond at her. Niida looked away.

All Camassans looked like ferns to her. She ate ferns, so had done her best to avoid Camassans, however nice they might be.

Niida watched Lula balance on her two legs. How had humans even survived with only two legs? Niida would have called it a design flaw.

"We'll begin this group with handing out assignments. In a couple of months, nearly half of the planet celebrates what humans call Christmas, even though few today celebrate it as a religious holiday.

"I thought it would be fun if we delved deep into one of the traditions of Christmas, since it's just over six weeks away. People used to sing what were called Christmas Carols to each other. One was called *The Twelve Days of Christmas.* Each day a number of gifts were sent to a true love. I'm going to assign you each a lyric to research and you will report back to the group what you think it means."